No part of this publication may be reproduced, stored in a retrieval system, or transmitted in any form or by any means, electronic, mechanical, photocopying, recording, scanning, or otherwise, without the prior written permission of the publisher, except in the case of brief quotations within critical reviews and otherwise as permitted by copyright law.

NOTE: This is a work of fiction. Names, characters, places, and incidents are a product of the author's imagination. Any resemblance to real life is purely coincidental. All characters in this story are 18 or older.

Copyright © 2021, Willow Winters Publishing. All rights reserved.

Delilah

Third of a Trilogy

USA TODAY BESTSELLING AUTHOR

USA Today best-selling author, Willow Winters, brings you an all-consuming, sizzling romance featuring an epic antihero you won't soon forget.

Some love stories are a slow burn. Others are quick to ignite, scorching and branding your very soul before you've taken that first breath. You're never given a chance to run from it.
That's how I'd describe what happened to us.

Everything around me blurred and all that existed were his lips, his touch ...
The chase and the heat between us became addictive.
Our nights together were a distraction, one we craved to the point of letting the world crumble around us.
We should have paid more attention; we should have known that it would come to this.
We both knew it couldn't last, but that didn't change what we desired most.
All we wanted was each other ...

This is the final book in the This Love Hurts trilogy.

This Love Hurts and *But I Need You* must be read first.

"It is sometimes an appropriate response to reality to go insane."

Philip K. Dick

To my readers who wonder,

"What happened to you that you write like this?"

I found others like me, and that was enough.

Prologue

Run. *Just run.*

The trees over the fence are brutal as their bark scratches down my right forearm. Branches whip at my face and I nearly impale myself on the spiked iron rail at the top of the fence before releasing it and dropping down. The hot blood smeared across my skin is more than enough evidence that damage has been done, but I don't even flinch. Dried leaves lash out at me as I scramble through the brush, the twigs littering the ground crunching beneath my feet as I fall.

Oof. Biting down on my lip I silence the cry that threatens to be ripped from me on impact. With a racing heart and tears pricking at my eyes, I force myself to move. I can't look back and I can't stop.

Everything's on fire, every weak muscle inside of me screaming with agonizing pain. I imagine this is what it's like to die, and that very thought keeps me moving.

Run. Just run.

The cries from the new boy are still vivid in my mind. It was only moments ago and I swear they still echo in my ears. His shrill scream rings clearly in my head, tainted by my heavy breathing as I draw in a lungful of air that's far too cold.

He won't last. They'll be back.

He should have run like me. The thought stays trapped at the back of my clogged throat as my bare feet almost slip on the damp grass before crossing onto the hard mud along the brick wall of some apartment building. I unlocked it. I tried to grab him but he only cried, whimpering on the floor and refusing to move.

My heart races as I glance one way and then the other.

For the first time since I swung the shovel, I stop. I stop for only a second, and his cries mix with another small boy's wail.

Marcus. The burn of tears is unmistakable now as they streak down my face. His voice haunts me still. The way he cried but tried not to ... I'll never forget it. I may be a child, but if I live through this, I know I'll never forget. Some memories are stained into who you are. The core of your soul is forever changed as a result.

My head is swarming with horrid memories and amid the nightmares is his smile, his consoling smile that everything would be all right. The images don't line up with the reality. His whispers that everything's going to be okay clash with the screams that prove it's not.

It's not all right. And it's because of me.

From somewhere deep within the weak voice whispers to run, but my small hand clings to the worn brick on the edge of the building I'm tucked behind. As if holding on to it will keep me from being seen. The tight grip doesn't allow me to escape. For a moment, I consider turning back and yelling at the boy I left behind. The door was unlocked and open. If he's still there ...

They'll kill him too. They'll do so much worse than that.

A staggered breath doesn't fulfill any need for oxygen. The memories suffocate me, knowing what they'll do if he doesn't run like I did. I can't move an inch in the freezing cold. The wind howls as I stare down a row of houses lining the quiet street.

In my mind, we were so far away from anyone who could help. But as I steady my breath, I see nothing but houses. I can't remember if we screamed for help, but I know we screamed in pain. If only I'd screamed louder. My chest is hollow and my head dizzy.

They were so close. So many people. Several cars are parked along the street.

One is missing a tire, and as I stare at it, my gaze is caught by two men perched on a stoop.

Like me, their hoodies practically swallow their lanky bodies, but the two men are tall and older. Just as I see them, they notice me. "Hey kid!" one calls out. He's got an unkempt beard streaked with enough white that I can see it from here, and a questioning gaze in his eyes.

Frozen and paralyzed, I don't speak until both of them stand. My mind struggles with the fact they're just on the other side of the street. They were so close. How could they have been so close?

"Are you all right?" The second man yells out the question before elbowing the other, and both of them start down the steps.

They're coming for me, but I don't know them. More importantly, they may have known. They could be lookouts for all I know.

"Kid, you okay? You need help?" they question, jogging across the street and heading right for me.

Some form of an answer begs to escape, but I can't respond. All I can think is that maybe they did hear, maybe they knew. Maybe they're going to send me back.

I can't think, I can't answer, I can't do anything but run.

I need to speak first, though. Just in case they're truly unaware, they need to know about the other boy, but the words don't come. How can I speak the truth when it kills me even to think of what happened?

I think of Marcus and what he'd say. He'd be brave enough.

My jaw is sore when I yell out, "The yellow house! They're in the yellow house on the corner!"

It's enough, just run!

The voice isn't my own and I take off as the two older men, only feet away, exchange puzzled glances. The alleyway is narrow, far too narrow for them to follow me, but I dart through the darkness, my bare feet stumbling over broken bottles, trash and muck. I would run through the fires of hell to get away, to be far away from all this.

I can't bear the thought of being back there and telling them what happened.

Telling them what I did and what happened because of it.

Run. Just run.

I run as far as I can. I run to what I thought was his home. I was wrong.

I was wrong about entirely too much.

Chapter 1

Cody

"You've got to be fucking shitting me," Skov hisses, slapping the papers off the steel table.

"That's what the lieutenant said." From where I sit in the steel chair, the shrug of Detective Gallinger's shoulders appears nonchalant. I know better.

I watch the two men argue in hushed tones, one standing in the hallway leading to the interrogation room and the former barely a foot inside. His white-knuckled grip on the door and bitter inflection have me on edge. Even if they're being forced to release me, Skov could pull some shit and keep me here. Trapped in this room, I'm useless. With every second that ticks by, all I can do is hope the door will burst open and someone will announce they've found Delilah. Half the time I imagine it, there's a sense of relief that follows. The other half of the time I've stared at the clock as these two cops drone on has led to me imagining they've found her lifeless body. All the while I did nothing to save her, because of them. My gaze narrows as I stare at the back of Skov's wrinkled button-down.

"It hasn't even been twenty-four hours yet." The statement comes out with a guttural groan from Detective Skov. He's a fucking idiot and so is his partner, Detective Gallinger, if either of them think I'm going to fall for this good cop, bad cop shtick. I'm an FBI agent, for fuck's sake.

There's only one piece of this act that's based on reality: Detective Skov wants me to go down for all of it. For every whisper of Marcus there's ever been. He's decided I am Marcus. That I created him and I've been the one responsible for the deeds attributed to Marcus. That part isn't entirely untrue. I'm responsible for more than anyone could possibly know. Even if they managed to find any evidence and could put the pieces together, there's so much that's gone unwritten. So many moments where I played a part in pawns being moved across the chessboard. The weight of that blame would have buried me alive over the past few hours if not for my constant monitoring of the clock while the names of men who could have possibly taken Delilah continued to pile up.

Skov's got a hunch I'm behind it all. He's made that more than clear. Even worse, he thinks Delilah's involved with

Marcus's crimes. The dull pain in my chest aches from rage every time he speaks her name. He should be searching every inch of Cadence's place with a fine-tooth comb. Looking for any evidence in the woods behind her apartment complex. Checking for any signs of a struggle from her mother who was also taken.

Anything at all other than wasting his time interrogating me and throwing out every accusation he can. If anything happens to Delilah, I'll murder them myself. All of them. The men who took her and the detectives who kept me in this cage so I couldn't go after her.

Picking at the dry skin on my knuckles, the two go back and forth over whether or not I should be released. Whether or not they can hold me against the lieutenant's orders. Whether or not the case is about to "break wide open."

As if I can't hear them over the groan of the ancient heater tucked into the drop ceiling above.

All the while, my frustration and anger simmers. I've sat here far too long, answering questions from men who know far too little. The weight of my sins pressing against my chest is heavy as I breathe in as deeply as I can, yet what's happened still feels suffocating.

They took her. My trembling hands find their way back onto the steel table, the metal feeling like ice against my heated flesh. My throat is raw and hoarse from screaming at the men who appear hell-bent on ending my career. Hours of fighting them, and for what? For nothing. Time is slipping away and I can do nothing to save her while I'm trapped here.

They have the wrong man, the wrong theory ... and all I can do is bite my tongue and pray to both God and the devil that Marcus already has her. I hope he tracked down the men who dared to take her and skinned them alive. With the back of my teeth grinding against one another, I silently wish he saves one of them for me. There's a bit of comfort in the thought that she's with him, safe and unharmed. More than a bit. I'd sell my soul for that to be reality.

The interrogation room door creaks as it opens further, allowing light from the hallway to drift into the dimly lit room. The fluorescent light above me hums and flickers, and it's then I realize how tired and dry my eyes are.

The temperature in the room is cranked up too high, uncomfortably so. After being awake for nearly twenty hours with no rest, I know their intention was to exhaust me and keep pushing until I crack and give them what they're looking for—answers about Marcus. My eyes are dry, itching and burning. Adrenaline, however, still pumps in my veins, so much so the very thought of sleep is nauseating.

"I'm going after your badge." Detective Skov's voice is barely heard as the details of what happened before my arrest play back in my mind. The phone call when everything was all right and then her chilling scream before the clatter of the phone dropping. The line went dead after that. She was there, then she was gone.

The detective continues even in my silence. As I rise, the legs of the chair scrape against the floor carelessly. "That reporter was onto something," he starts, and I vaguely recall Jill Brown and her accusations. "And I don't care if I spend the rest of my career getting to the bottom of it."

"Can I go?"

Skov's dark gaze narrows with his jaw clenched tight. It's Gallinger who answers, "Yes."

Thud, thud, thud, my heart races, the adrenaline in my veins somehow increasing and forcing an anxiousness to overwhelm me. I need to find her.

"There's not enough evidence." Gallinger continues to talk although I'm barely listening as I gather my coat and walk out. His black boot finds the painted cream brick of the wall behind him as he leans against it. "If you have any intel," he says, raising his voice so I can hear more easily, as if I haven't been listening all the while like they intended, "you'll fill us in, won't you?" His thick eyebrows lift in question.

"I don't trust you, I don't like you, and I'm going to destroy you," the detective I've left behind mutters beneath his breath, but it's loud enough to be heard.

"Fuck both of you." My response is as dull as the fucks I give when it comes to these two. The glares from each of them burn into my skin as I walk as casually as I can down the hallway.

"This way, Agent—"

"I know where to go," I say, brushing aside the officer in charge of escorting me to the front to collect my belongings.

"This is the last time I let you walk out of here," the prick of a detective calls out after me. There's an audience of sorts at the end of the hallway: three officers, one with a cuffed man who appears homeless sitting on the bench against the back wall, and the other two pushing papers around.

Blinking away the pain in my sore eyes, I barely read that it's nine in the morning. Too many hours have already passed, and it'll take another twenty minutes to fill out paperwork and get the hell out of here.

The process is painfully slow, and the entire time my conscience is plagued by sounds of that phone call. One minute she was there, the next she was gone.

The bastards took their time. An hour of waiting, followed by the thirty minutes it took to hail a cab and be taken back to my car. All the while my mind was screaming. They know the same as I do: the first seventy-two hours are crucial. And yet they chose to spend the better part of the first twenty-four hours interrogating me.

Anger consumes me as I face the cold hard truth: either they don't believe she was taken, or they think I've murdered her.

There is no other explanation.

Glancing in the rearview mirror, the sight of my reddened gaze brings my fatigue front and center. I rub my eyes with the heel of my palms to no avail. I can't blink away the last day and a half, let alone the last two decades.

It's all my fault. With every slow blink, I picture Delilah and all the times we had where nothing else mattered. It all melted away when I was with her. She was an escape and I lost myself in her company. I think about the last time we were together, imagining the sight of her pouty lips with her top teeth digging into her bottom lip as she moaned. The feel of her silky ebony hair as her neck arched in ecstasy, allowing the stray strands to brush against my bare skin. With a deep inhale I let the memories take me away. Even something as simple as the smell of her caramel skin allowed me to slip away from the chaos and into her bed.

The honk of cars behind me is the only reason I come back to reality, forced to stare back at a now green light. Forced to move forward, but having no fucking clue where to go.

I need Marcus. For the first time in my life, I truly need him. This isn't a vendetta or vigilante mission. This isn't searching out justice when the system failed.

This is so much more. This is righting my wrong and saving an innocent before it's too late. I shouldn't have touched her and brought her into this. I should have known better.

The busy street blurs as I glance between my phone and

the rearview again. My brow pinches and, shortly after, a prickling sensation travels from the base of my skull all the way down my spine.

A white sedan has trailed two cars behind me for miles now, even though the two vehicles between us have changed periodically. Whoever it is has kept their distance but followed ever since I left the station. I'm sure of it.

The clicks of my blinker resound like a ticking clock. Although I'm not certain what will greet me when the pendulum stops.

The car follows, not bothering to wait for more than ten seconds. It's definitely a tail. My right hand forms a fist, one that pounds once on the leather wheel in frustration. It's the fucking detectives. As if the situation couldn't get any worse. I can't make out the driver, but my gut tells me it's more than likely Skov.

Pressing the pedal down, I don't waste a moment, cutting off the car next to me and veering right across two lanes. The exit isn't for another two miles. I only take my eyes off the road, the speedometer revving, to ensure the white car gives chase. Recklessly it does and the driver, wearing large sunglasses that cover most of his face, nearly crashes into a minivan that can't slow fast enough to accommodate. With the act comes a screech of tires. More horns blare. I'm sure he's aware his cover is blown, and he barely manages to squeeze into the rightmost lane.

I use the loss of momentum due to traffic and cut my wheel hard to the left, where the exit is only a block away. My phone on the passenger seat smashes into the dashboard, while whatever's behind me slams against the back of my seat.

Adrenaline pumps hard, so hard my throat feels tight with the pressure of my racing pulse. All I can hear is the blood rushing in my ears.

The driver of the black coupe I cut off lays on his horn and slams on his brakes, which gives me plenty of room to make it to the exit as I leave the tail behind, still caught between cars a lane over.

Rounding the bend of the exit, it takes longer than it should for the panic to subside. My eyes track every car that surrounds me on the interstate from the rearview.

It's only once I'm sure I've lost him that I start to doubt who was behind the wheel.

It could be the cops. Or it could be someone helping whoever took Delilah. Fear and anger swirl into a deadly concoction in the pit of my stomach.

Even minutes later, the dominant feeling that remains is still dread.

Twisting my sweaty palms around the steering wheel, I readjust my grip when I'm certain there's no one else following me.

Guilt and shame are next to greet me, slipping in as the trepidation wanes.

Marcus's words resonate in the darkness of my mind: *It's my fault.*

They took her when it was my watch. I should have been there. I shouldn't have given her space. I was supposed to protect her.

If I could go back, I never would have returned her kiss. I never would have given into temptation. I've been in too deep with Marcus for far too long to think it wasn't going to catch up with me. There's not a doubt in my mind that this is all related to someone I fucked over.

Not knowing who's following me, I come to the conclusion that I need to be careful with every step. I can't leave a trail for anyone to follow. I need to call Marcus, but certainly not with my cell which still lays on the floor of the passenger seat. My head shakes as I see the screen split in two with a jagged crack down the center.

It takes twenty minutes, heading in the opposite direction of the hotel room I was staying at when Delilah was taken, to reach a pay phone in a corner lot of a strip mall.

I know the number to call by heart. Marcus had a habit of changing the numbers he used, but he always went back to the first one we ever spoke on. For the first year the only ways we communicated were through letters and notes left at crime scenes. The year after is when he called me for the first time and I finally heard his voice. It broke me to hear the voice of my brother, grown into a man and disguising it on the other end. That was the year I met Delilah too. I suppose she's always been a part of it.

I stared at the phone, memorizing the number he called me from while his voice burned into my mind.

It killed me in my soul to know for certain what my brother had become. How could he have thought I wouldn't recognize his voice? His mannerisms and the way he paused between words were identical to the voice of a gleeful child. It's odd to realize how unique a person's speech is. For years I listened to a saved voicemail that was only fifty-three seconds long. It was a birthday message and the only recording I had of my little brother. None of the fine details and idiosyncrasies in his voice escaped me over time.

I dial the number now, each press on the small metal keypad chilling my middle finger as I do.

It rings and rings, seemingly in slow motion. The cars pass, and in the distance someone calls out to another person ahead of them. All of the noises distort around me before fading to white noise, but the harsh ring of the phone not being picked up is what stays with me. The click of an unanswered call carries a sense of finality and foreboding.

With a trembling hand, I dial the number again. Marcus has used it dozens of times with me over the years. He used to go back and forth between this one and new numbers. I wrote each one down every time he called, searching for a pattern and some way to find him. He always went back to this phone number. It's the only one he repeated.

Ring, ring, ring.

Nothing. Nothing at all.

I try again. And again there's nothing.

With a sinking feeling in my gut, I swallow thickly and call once more.

With thick clouds gathering above me, the gray soon blocks out the sun and the sky is shattered as lightning strikes, preceding the rumble of thunder in the distance.

Again ... nothing.

Staring at the pay phone, I hesitate to leave it. If I could leave a message, I would. A plea for him to tell me she's all right. Even if he were to never let me see her again. Even if he never spoke to me again.

To simply know he has her would ease the sickening feeling that threatens to overwhelm me as I set the handset back where it belongs.

With my limbs heavy and the darkness coming, I head back to my car in time to hear my cell phone ring. Hope is an awful thing, and it's shattered as quickly as it came. It's only Evan, a member of my team.

Back when I had a team, that is. There's no doubt I'll be forced to take leave.

Another wave of guilt and shame makes my stomach drop as I realize that's more than likely why he's calling. He's giving me a heads-up.

The phone continues to ring in my hand and I let it.

I can't answer. What could I possibly say? What truth could I provide right now that wouldn't morph into yet another lie?

Only a moment after the vibration stops does another come, indicating a voicemail.

I can barely stand to look at it. Evan has been my right-hand man and the closest partner I've had on the team for years. He was practically my mentor. I've killed for him and he's done the same for me. Yet here I am, hiding and knowing damn well he'd never understand. There's no justification for bringing Delilah into this shit. Let alone what I've done with Marcus. There's no way to confide in him about Delilah without also confessing the truth about Marcus. The three of us are tied together, our histories unable to be separated.

Rolling down the window, the bitter wind strikes my face and I let it. The brutality is nothing compared to what I deserve. My only options are Marcus, who won't answer the damn phone, or lying to my partner. My eyes creep open slowly, the tiredness intensified by the chill in the air, yet all of it muted as I realize I can lie so well. All I truly need to tell Evan is what I heard on the other end of the line when Delilah was taken. I don't have to tell him everything. All I have to do is tell him I need help finding her.

If I had no other information, no other insight at all, what would I be able to tell him? What needs to be omitted?

The wheels turn and a sense of control takes over. For the first time since I've left that godforsaken interrogation room, a different sensation comes over me. Evan will believe me. He'll help me even in the face of knowing it would need to be kept quiet. At the very least, I can use him to find out any information that would possibly lead me to Delilah.

Chapter 2

Delilah

I don't know how long I've slept, but it must be twenty-four hours that have passed. At least a day, maybe two. The hopelessness is nothing compared to the terror every time I think I hear something. There's some kind of piping above this room. The sound of water rushes in and out occasionally. The cracked cement floor of this ten-by-ten-foot cell reeks of urine and it's stained with blood. The brick walls are old and crumbled in places where it appears that others have attempted to escape. Beneath one broken section, discolored with what I imagine is blood from the fingers of someone prying the stones apart with their bare hands, is yet another layer of brick.

Without a single window, I have no idea where I am or

whether or not my screams can even be heard.

Pain strikes my body and spikes with every small movement, from my puffy and split lips that leave the tang of blood in my mouth every time I try to part it, to my ribs that I think are bruised or broken. If I breathe too deep ... it's excruciating to the point that my body doubles over. It only makes the agony even worse.

The voices of victims have stayed with me, haunting me in the quiet hours that have passed. Their recollections of the madness and panic when they were taken and held in various prisons play over and over again.

Women who confessed their testimonies to me in between sobs with tears streaking down their faces, clinging to the truth they thought they'd die in those cells, whisper their stories to me here. Just as I did in my bed on so many late nights when I heard what they'd gone through, I cry for them and pretend I'm not crying for myself as well.

I've barely slept. Given how dry and sore my eyes are, I doubt I've blinked more than physically necessary since I woke up last. All I can do is stare at the steel door, dinged and battered with rust covering its surface. Unlike me, it belongs in this place.

If I could bear to sit up, I'd test the hinges and attempt to pry one out ... *as if I could possibly budge the iron with just my hands ...* I huff sarcastically at the thought, and the small movement causes me to wince with pain. As it is, I lie here on the cold hard ground, staring at the door and attempting to recollect what happened, trying to recall if there were any clues at all.

I have none, though. They were silent. They wore masks. Even when they stuck me in what I think was a van or a bus, something large enough for me to nearly stand in when I woke screaming, even then, they were silent. There was no radio, there was no indication of anything. With a bag over my head and my wrists bound as I was transported here, I have no evidence or inkling whatsoever of where I am.

Moreover, the list of those who'd want me dead or ransomed, or simply out of the picture has grown in my mind.

Men I've put in prison who may have been released.

Enemies of Special Agent Walsh ... rivals of Marcus.

With the reports and articles released months ago that continued to spew lies about my intentions and abilities with the cold cases, even the mourning, innocent family and friends of victims may wish for my death if they believe Jill Brown and the accusations she threw at me.

When my memory isn't flooded with previous cases, and my mind isn't examining lists and motives, my subconscious drifts to a more peaceful place. To hope that two men will find me. Marcus and Cody.

Picking at a broken nail, emotions swim up my throat and I force them down with a harsh swallow. My tired eyes drift shut and I see the two of them. A warmth covers my chilled skin and, for a moment, I'm blanketed by the familiar, unmistakable scent of a certain man. His breath on my neck, his lips teasing mine as he lays me down in bed. Marcus's hand slips lower and he soothes the pain.

My eyes open slowly, the vision fading in front of me as I come to terms with reality.

Never once did I think of myself as a princess locked in a tower and waiting on her prince when I was younger. Never did I play the part of damsel in distress. This isn't a fairytale; my princes lie and cheat and kill. They hide in dark corners and play vicious games with violent men.

Sniffling, I wonder, what's the likelihood they'll come save me? What information could possibly lead them here? Is there any indication of who took me?

Given the time that's passed, my gut sinks and any sense of peace or hope is shattered. If they knew where I was, they would be here by now.

Assuming they had any intention of coming for me.

What keeps me from thinking the worst is that they're out there, somewhere beyond the confines of this cell where evidence can be found. I'm stuck in here without a single clue.

If I could have given Cody information in that split second I turned around, it would have been that the man was at least six feet, and tanned skin peeked out from the gap between the sleeves of the black sweater and gloves he wore. Not an inch of his face was recognizable, but dark eyes stared back at me from the slit in his mask. His expression was angry and unforgiving.

The only saving grace I have is that my face was covered as well, my vision obscured the entire time. That is the only piece of this puzzle that offers me any hint of reprieve. They didn't want me to see them, which means perhaps they'll let me live.

Fate laughs a wretched sound at the thought. The one thread of hope is instantly stripped away from me when a man I recognize all too well appears in the place of the steel door. It opens with a slow creak and as I heave in the air, two men, masked just the same as the one who first struck me, stand behind him.

"Miss Jones." Brass's cadence is sickeningly sweet. He greets me as if we're old friends. "It's been too long, don't you think?" He's the shortest of the three and unarmed, although the two men behind him who are broader and more muscular, each hold a rifle in their hands.

Hired help? My mind whirls with connections and associates. But names mix together and cases bleed into one another as exhaustion and fear work against me.

"Miss Jones?" he repeats and I force my tired eyes up to meet his icy gaze. Herman and Reynolds. The two names linked to Brass ring clearly in my head, and faces are paired with photos of the criminals who got off. The three of them worked together, laundering money and diving into deeper, more sordid crimes. That's what men do when they have wealth, they indulge in sin and those three together ... bile threatens to climb up my throat. Herman's dead now. I'm fairly sure Marcus killed him because of the threatening note left for me at my office door; everything is circumstantial, though. Herman did have a team who worked with Reynolds. And Reynolds certainly worked with Brass. Does this all have to do with the note? Or with Herman's murder?

Brass's teeth are far too perfect, too even and white as he flashes me a crooked grin, the left side of his smile higher than the right. He huffs a laugh and half-heartedly looks behind him at the two men, who stay perfectly still and silent. I stare hard at the other two men, but I'm not certain one could be Reynolds. Perhaps these two are working for them, but their heights and silence don't match what I know of Reynolds, or at least what I can remember.

Cases flutter in my mind as Brass stalks toward me. The men stay where they are, and the door remains open. I suppose they're here for intimidation. Ross Brass always was a bit of a repulsive, slimy prick.

I'm not his usual victim. Brief images of the young girls he's responsible for the deaths of send a chill down my spine. I'm too old for his liking. So this is all about revenge, or maybe it's a threat.

Please, God, let this be a threat and only that.

"I said, hasn't it been too long?" Impatience lingers in

his question.

"Not long enough," I manage to answer, ignoring the vicious pain that radiates up my neck and travels down my shoulders as I raise my head to meet his gaze. My own is as hard and cold as ice.

The humor and obvious satisfaction that graced his expression a moment ago falters slightly at my response.

"I had a number of names on the list of vile criminals who could have taken me, but to be honest, you kidnapping me ... murdering me ... whatever this is," I say, then half-heartedly attempt a nonchalant gesture. As I do, the back of my teeth slam shut and grind as I swallow down the nearly unbearable pain. I attempt a huff of laughter myself and add, "Well, I didn't even think you cared that much."

The anger that lights in the flecks of amber dotting his irises is exactly what I'm after. I need him off guard, I need him reckless so I can get any information at all from him. "What exactly is this?" I dare to question as his nostrils flare.

His posture stiffens as his hands slip into the pockets of his black suit pants. His white button-down is crisp, and his thin, black tie dangles in front of him as he paces along the wall opposite from me, seemingly checking every inch of my prison.

In some ways, his stature and clothing are out of place in this shithole. In other ways, though, a man like him belongs here. It's like a piece of him feels right at home and there's an air about him that confirms it.

"What is this?" he hisses, echoing my question and a chill runs down the length of my body when he smiles thinly and says, "It's called revenge. We had a deal."

"A deal?"

"Not with you," he adds and the coldness penetrates my skin, seeping down deep. If it isn't about me, then taking control of the situation is out of my reach.

"Then with who?" I manage to speak, although my question is shaky.

A snort of a laugh leaves him, and his right hand slips out of his pocket so he can run his thumb along the stubble covering his jaw. "I almost feel sorry for you."

"Why on earth would anyone feel sorry for me?" I respond morosely but as I do, the pain gets the best of me and whatever false armor I wore cracks around me. Even worse, Brass sees it.

With his back to me, Brass doesn't answer me as he signals for the two men to leave, but what he says next gives me one more piece of the puzzle before following behind them:

"He interfered and took what was rightfully mine, so I'm taking what's his."

CHAPTER 3

CODY

As I lean forward in the cheap chair planted in the corner, heat rolls down my shoulders. It's an anxiousness that doesn't quit and leads my foot to *tap, tap, tap* on the rug below. I've debated even being here in this hotel room. According to Evan, I've been told to go home and stay there. It's an unofficial house arrest from my superiors.

That's hours away from where Delilah was taken, though.

My home address is where the two detectives will go first if they find any evidence that can lead to yet another arrest. They've been informed of the decision to send me home and keep me off the case. Courtesy of Evan himself. With Skov hell-bent on pinning this all on me, I'm certain he'll demand he be the one to take me in. It'll give him some sick sense of satisfaction.

Clearing my throat, I force myself to lean back and then rub my sore eyes with the heel of my palms before checking my phone again. It's habitual. Between the articles I've flicked through on my laptop and the texts on my phone, I'm going crazy from the waiting.

Evan still hasn't messaged since he told me he was looking into a lead and to stay here. Delilah stayed here before. Not this room, but here in this hotel.

I have to force myself to stop thinking of her. I covered every inch of her sister's place and left no stone unturned. I searched it up and down and found nothing.

Evan wouldn't give me all the details over the phone, and at first it pissed me off. Now it's left me with a churning feeling deep in the pit of my stomach. I'm not sure what he had a lead on or where it will take him, but he knows where I am. He knows, and now Marcus knows since I left him a message. Delilah's sister knows too as I reached out to her, telling her I'm an investigator on her sister's case, needing to get any information I could, but only reached a voicemail.

Every trail has led to a dead end.

What's to come is uncertain, and without control and without allies … without knowing Delilah is still alive, it feels as if death has its grip on my shoulders. Holding me down and forcing me to watch as the devil strips everything from me, claiming his pay for my sins.

Knock, knock, knock.

The thuds on the door aren't gentle or expected, and instinctively, my right hand jolts to my gun on the side table. Until I hear her voice.

"Special Agent Cody Walsh?" She knocks again. "Are you in there? Please! It's about my sister."

Delilah introduced me to her sister years ago, but it still takes me a moment to realize it's her sister. The rhythm and subtle inflections in her tone mimic Delilah's. The ache that travels through my chest is undeniable.

If only Delilah would knock on my door. If only it was all a misunderstanding.

I'm silent but swift as I rise, eager to find out if her sister knows anything at all. I've read through the reports a dozen times. She gave her statement and, in those lines, she didn't know a damn thing that could help. If she does, she isn't aware of it. The details she doesn't think are important are the ones I'm after. The ones she didn't think were worth mentioning.

Her small hand is fisted and prepared for another rap against the door, her lips parted and ready to call out once again when I open the hotel door.

Her deep brown eyes widen at the sight of me, and her mouth slams shut. It's only then I realize I must appear disheveled at best. Unhinged at worst.

"I ... I didn't mean to wake you."

You didn't. The answer stays glued to my tongue. I still haven't slept. It's going on thirty-six hours since Delilah was taken, and I'm still wearing the wrinkled trousers and the shirt I was in when I got the call.

Cadence's gaze travels lower, noting that I'm not in sleepwear.

Tightening her cream wool coat around her waist, she straightens her shoulders to state, although it's more of a plea, "I need to talk to you."

"Come in." My answer is raspy and I find myself clearing my throat as I open the door wider for her.

She's halfway into the room, staring between the bed and the chair in the corner when I start by saying, "I read your statement. Have you remembered anything since you gave it?"

I hesitate to do it, but I lock the door before offering her a weak smile. "I don't want to make you uncomfortable—"

"No, please." Inhaling deeply, she drops her coat to the middle of the bed and then takes a seat on the edge. "After what happened," she says and her voice drifts off, leaving the statement unfinished.

"Right." I give her a small nod and resume my place in the corner chair, turning it to face her. "Have you remembered anything?"

"I came to ask you questions," Cadence blurts out, nearly interrupting my question, a hint of skepticism in her tone. After a second, she huffs a humorless laugh that doesn't reach her eyes. With a frown pulling down the corners of her lips, she wipes the edges of her eyes with the sleeve of her deep ruby designer sweater. "Sorry," she says. "I just ... I have questions."

Staring back at Delilah's sister, seeing every resemblance I can find in the woman across the room, I offer her another smile, although this one is weaker. "You remind me of her."

Cadence's smile is tight but genuine, and dampened by the pain in her eyes. "So you remember me, don't you?"

With a nod, I answer, "I do. Cadence Jones, Delilah's sister. We met years ago."

"I know you were seeing her." Her statement catches me off guard.

"I didn't know she told anyone."

"It was all over the papers," she confesses. "I read about your so-called affair. Pair that with her limited free time ... well I assumed she'd met someone."

I can only nod, remembering the beginning of ... whatever we were. With a tight throat, sadness rocks through me.

"So I have questions."

"Of course you do," I respond lowly.

"And I'm sure you know ... statistically speaking, when someone is in a relationship and taken or—"

"I know the partner is the first suspect. Lover or husband." My tone turns colder as Marcus comes to mind. Clearing my throat again, I lean forward and reach for the tumbler on the table, only to find the whiskey's been drained from it. "I love her and I'm going to find her," I say with every intention of upholding my vow until I glance down, from Cadence's hopeful gaze, to the laptop screen that's turned black.

Hopelessness is a traitor. "Would you like anything to drink?"

Cadence only shakes her head, not a hair out of place in her bun as she does so. It's at odds with her face, completely devoid of makeup other than traces of mascara around her eyes, which only adds to the darkness beneath them.

"It's the second day." Her voice cracks and it resonates in my chest. "Please tell me you know something." Her plea morphs into a whisper, the almost palpable sadness overwhelming it.

The only words I have for her are, "I'm sorry," but I refuse to say them. It's what I've told the loved ones of bodies I've found, all the men, women and children who weren't found alive. I can't do that to Delilah. I won't utter a statement that echoes defeat.

"We're going to find her."

"I was hoping you would tell me it wasn't real." Cadence's expression crumples. "After my mother's body—" Her statement is left unfinished, but I know what she's referring to. The news covered it and Evan sent me the report. Her death was quick.

"I'm sorry about your mother," I say, offering my

condolences, wishing I'd spoken them sooner.

Her eyes glaze over and her shoulders hunch forward as she stifles a sob. "I'm sorry." Her apology is barely heard as she reaches into her purse, pulling out tissues.

If I could comfort her, I would, but I don't want to approach her. I've never been the best at soothing someone else's pain. My uncle made a point to tell me that fact frequently.

"Let me get you a bottle of water," I offer and stand, making my way to the room's small fridge and pulling out one of three that remain. The whiskey on the laminate desk stares at me, the amber liquid sloshing as I close the fridge door.

"Thank you." Her voice is weak, so much smaller than it was a moment ago.

She's still sipping on it when I've retaken my seat.

"What questions do you have?" I ask her to move this along.

"Do you know who took her?"

"No."

"What can you tell me?" My chest aches as she searches for any information at all.

"I wish I could give you answers. But I called you for them because I don't have any."

With trembling hands, her gaze moves to her lap and it's quiet for far too long. More than a moment passes with Cadence visibly distraught and neither of us having any new information for the other.

Just when I think she'll stand to leave, she leans forward

with a look of uncertainty on her face. "There's something I have to tell you." Her tone is deadly serious. "I couldn't tell the cops."

"You can tell me anything." Although it's the truth, the statement comes out too eagerly and she hesitates, but gives in. More than likely due to having no other options.

"There is no man who killed my father. My mother killed him. So it couldn't have been Marcus or whoever the police are claiming killed him."

I already know. Delilah didn't tell me, but Marcus did in so many words.

Debating whether or not I should feign ignorance doesn't last long. Instead I lie. "I know. She told me."

Shock lights her eyes and I can see it from across the room. "Did she tell you why?"

"No." I haven't the faintest idea why her mother did what she did. All Marcus hinted at was that it was deserved.

"My father wasn't a good man."

"Good men and bad men, it's not quite as well defined of a line as I once thought it was."

"What do you know about my father? Because there's no gray about it. Only black and white."

"Only what Delilah told me."

She huffs sarcastically. "He was her hero, so I'm sure she didn't tell you the truth."

"And what's the truth?"

"He was a liar." She's quick to answer. "I knew him to be a liar and a thief at times. I knew him to be ... cruel."

As I turn to glance at the clock, Cadence sees and her strength leaves her.

"Delilah never knew, but our mother had just cause for what she did as far as I'm concerned."

"Delilah never knew what?"

"She never knew what kind of man he was." She swallows thickly, the sound eating up the silence. "It's strange how she doesn't remember. How he was her hero, yet he was my villain, all in the same scene."

"He hurt her?" I surmise. "He hurt your mother?" She only nods in answer and reaches again for the bottle of water.

"Did he ever hurt you?"

"Not directly, but that doesn't mean it didn't hurt me."

"Whoever has your sister ... I don't think it has anything to do with your father or your mother," I tell her honestly.

"I know ... but why would anyone go after her? Is it the threat? This Marcus?" She doesn't contain the exasperation clearly getting the best of her. She needs answers, but don't we all? "Brass or whoever it was who left that note in her office? Who? Who!"

It takes great effort to keep my expression unmoving as she lists suspects and tells me her theories.

Neither of us make any progress. We can't help each other, and that truth is evident to both of us before the hour is through.

"I came to tell you I don't think it's Marcus and to look somewhere else. The cops think it's Marcus, which is ridiculous."

"What do you mean? Who told you that?"

"That detective with the beard ... Skov. I told him Marcus doesn't exist, it's just a name used as a cover," she says incredulously and I can't fix my expression fast enough. With a tilt of her head, I can tell she knows that I know something about Marcus.

I want to tell her; I want to confess everything. If for no other reason than to rid myself of the burden of these sins and lies. They've piled up and now they're drowning me.

I still don't know who has Delilah. I don't know how to get her back. But I know it's because of myself and Marcus. It's because I couldn't walk away from her.

Because I brought her into something that was slowly killing me.

"What do you know? She told me Marcus wasn't real. I asked her, and she told me it was just a name whispered by liars to hide evidence."

"When was that?" I can't help but to question, and her gaze narrows.

"Years ago. I told the cops there's someone else behind those murders. It isn't one man, and Delilah told me that years ago."

"I don't know about that." I decide right then to hide behind lies. She can't be brought into this.

"What do you know?" she asks with a look of ridicule.

"Nothing, but you need to stop this. You need to stay away and let us do our job."

Shaking her head, she stands abruptly, anger taking over. "I can't—"

"You need to stay far away," I say, cutting her off, striding to the door of the hotel in an instant and opening the door as wide as it'll go.

"I mean it, Cadence." I warn her like I should have warned her sister, regret lacing each word, "Stay far away."

Chapter 4

Marcus

Fifteen years ago
Six years after abduction

They're all pawns.

I trace over the words at the top of the page in my notebook: *They're all pawns.* Writing down three more names to the list on the rightmost side of the yellowed pad with deep strokes of the blue ink pen, I pause to look at the tally.

There are three columns and over fifty names total. Three different groups of men, but all of them responsible for atrocities in the name of unity and solidarity. Everywhere I've gone there are always dogs like the ones I trailed today. Men, and even women, who go along with the men in power and do their bidding *without question. It doesn't take much to get them to move. A nod, a promise of ambition, and the desire for one man to have something done.*

He never says how. The men in charge never give those details, and that's why I've deemed the ones on the lists under the underlined names dogs. *They're owned by the men in charge, happily wagging their tails and barking orders to others as if they have any status in the pack at all. Snarling and backing the weaker ones into corners, they're as moldable as they are feral.*

The three kingpins, including Talvery, a crime family boss in this area, can't be bent or broken. But the men beneath them could easily be swayed. Or put in a ring and made to fight one another.

I haven't decided which is best yet. All I know is that there are plenty of pawns to play with. Plenty of them to start the game and deliver justice piece by piece.

The snap of a twig beneath heavy feet rips my gaze from the three names I've added. The graveyard is a scenery of grays and greens. The stones and the oak trees and the grass, long overdue for a cut, nearly hide the one I've been waiting for.

His name is inconsequential. What matters is the fact that his sister was a bird.

Another twig cracks under his weight as he comes into view. All of the burial plots surrounding where he stands are covered with time. The one at his feet, however, is marked by fresh blades of grass and overturned dirt.

A month has passed, but spring has only just begun. I don't think he's noticed me, and I stay quiet, merely observing him as I have for months. All I've done is watched. If Mr. Jones taught me anything at all, it's to take it all in, every detail, and to learn the habits of whoever it is that's selected. Mr. Jones chooses victims. I don't lower myself to his level, and I promised myself I never would. I don't think I'll be seeing much of him anymore. Not after I left him the note. I've never seen so much damage caused by a simple letter.

Smiling at the thought, I close my notebook and take in the boy I've been waiting for.

Charlie, the thin boy in worn jeans and a dark hoodie stares straight ahead, seemingly at nothing. He still hasn't dropped the flowers he brought. He does this when he works the day shift at the garage. The sun setting is the only reason he leaves. One might say he's guilt ridden and for good reason.

He sits feet from me, but still fails to realize he's not alone, at a grave with an inscription that reads:

When you are not fed love on a silver spoon, you learn to lick it off knives. ~ Lauren Eden

Although, that's not the woman's name carved on the tombstone.

"You okay?" I speak up without walking toward him, still leaning against the tree. After an initial shudder of shock, with his grip tight around the bouquet, Charlie's gaze meets mine. It's easy to tell I scared him at first. He's been afraid ever since

they killed her.

"Yeah, just ... Yeah, I'm fine," *he says, then offers me a tight smile and finishes the thought.* "Just leaving flowers."

"For who?" *I play up my youth. I know I look younger than I am. Poor nutrition will do that.*

"My sister."

All men are fueled by motives, by desires. Revenge is a deep-seated motive. We all have it buried inside of us. Including a high school boy, burdened by his mother's poor choices and his sister's death.

"What happened to her?" I chance a couple steps closer, eyeing the grave as if I haven't seen it a dozen times before.

A gust of wind blows by, followed by silence. In the last few weeks, Charlie's told four people what happened. He broke down at his workplace, the garage. He's been slipping away and devolving. I nearly second-guess my decision to approach him today, the two-month anniversary of her death, and the two-week anniversary of the man who killed her getting off scot-free.

But then he answers, "She got involved with the wrong kind of people."

"The wrong kind of people?" I know damn well who his sister was and the relationships he's referring to. Knowledge is the only path that will save the damned.

"Yeah ... they weren't good guys." He swallows thickly and his reddened cheeks burn brighter as he closes his eyes and allows the wind to batter him. "She said she was seeing ... someone." He shakes his head, huffing out a humorless breath and says, "Sorry, kid. I didn't mean to—"

"My mother says it's best to talk if you can," I lie. I barely think of my mother anymore. Or my father. "So if you want to talk, I can listen," I say, taking a seat on the stump of a tree closer to him but still at a distance. The stump isn't a product of a saw. It wasn't cut down; the bark is torn and the rings rough and jagged beneath my ass from where a storm long ago brought down the old tree.

"What are you, like ... eleven?"

"Fifteen," I tell him and smile. Charlie, the brother of Elizabeth Riggins, is almost twenty. He stayed in his hometown of Fallbrook to be close to his mother, and I imagine her hands dig deep in his pockets with that very hug he offers her each time she gives him a sob story. A broken home and a drug addiction aren't uncommon around here. It's a prime location for dogs to run free.

"So she fell in love with the wrong guy? It's like Romeo and Juliet." I speak nonsense, now seated lower than him so he's forced to look down at me. Pulling an apple from my jacket pocket, I bite into it watching as he shakes his head yet again.

Charlie Riggins will think me a young fool, but I know him for what he is. A young man at the precipice of who he'll become. He's mourning and barely holding back a smoldering fire that burns within.

"Romeo he was not, kid."

I smile every time they call me kid. They always do that. Children aren't threatening and they don't understand. That's their first mistake.

"He was a bad man," Charlie comments with his gaze settling on the cuts in the stone. His fingers trace over the quote. I'd planned on asking him what it meant, but silence holds back my swallow, the fresh apple tasting like the corrupt fruit it is instead.

Bad men always lose. A voice I only hear at night whispers that fact to me.

"So what are you going to do about it?" I ask Charlie, nearly choking as I swallow.

"Do about what?" he says with all sincerity.

"About the man who killed your sister?"

"I don't know that he killed her." The hair on the back of my neck stands on end; I didn't expect him to lie to me. He knows he killed her. Even if he doesn't have the proof I have, he knows.

"You blame him, though?"

"Yeah … he took her—it doesn't matter." He stops himself from saying more, not wanting to tell me she was last seen getting into the car with him. Plenty of witnesses saw them fighting, although they don't know what they were fighting over. It's the same thing it always is. Money.

Finley stole from his boss and she saw the money, took

it and spent it. Addiction will make you do stupid things. Finley killed her to save his own ass with the boss.

He's a dog and I have a plan for him. A plan that involves Charlie.

"There's a guy I've heard of. His name is Marcus." I tell him the story I've developed and worked out over the last few months. "I think he knows a lot of bad guys, and I think he wants them dead."

"Dead?" Charlie sounds shocked I'd use that word. Although I can feel his gaze on me, I don't look back up at him.

"He said they deserve to die," I say before taking another bite of the apple, although this time, it tastes sweeter.

"Oh yeah?"

He doesn't take me seriously. They never do.

"Yeah, he killed a bunch of Talvery's guys last week."

That gets Charlie's attention. The atmosphere turns darker as the sun falls behind the tree line. Soon it will be nearly pitch black under this canopy. I don't have much time left to convince him.

"I've heard if you pray at the graveyard, he hears. That's why I'm here. I wanted to pray."

Goosebumps and the chills that come with my story are an added blessing. The wind whips by and Charlie slips his hands into his hoodie's pockets, still refusing to take his concerned eyes off of me. I can practically see the wheels spin in his head as he contemplates Finley's death. Praying for a justice that he knows damn well he'll never get otherwise.

"What are you praying for?" he asks me and I finally meet his gaze when I answer, "That the men who hurt us get what they have coming to them."

The coldness swirls around me and another minute passes, the night sky getting darker. Charlie arches his neck, looking up at the canopy of leaves as if asking them a question.

"What's your name, kid?"

"Marcus says I shouldn't tell strangers my name," I'm quick to respond, and I can tell he doesn't like that answer.

With his head tilted he questions, "You know this Marcus well?"

"I've spoken to him once."

"How'd you do that? Praying and waiting for an answer?"

"Why? Do you want me to give him a message? The last guy did. I don't mind being the pigeon. Birds are good, he says. It's the dogs that are bad."

Present time

It surprises me how many times I've overheard conversations discussing the difference between light and dark. It's written in poetry and plays. It's presented as if it's fact. As if truth can't be seen in shadows. As if clarity does not shine on the depths of sin within each of us. There is no forgiveness that comes simply because the sun has risen. It is not so easy, nor so simple.

The only difference between light and dark is what our eyes have adjusted to. What we choose to see and believe. The reality is that nothing changes solely because of the amount of light we let in. Anger has always continued to rise anew regardless of every time a person smiles and states some charming line about the sun always coming out after rain, or sings a lyric describing making it through the night.

I've often thought I hold that opinion because of the cells we were kept in. We could never tell if it was night or day. There was constant little light in an ever-present darkness. Even in the barn, the day would blur with the night because I often couldn't sleep through either.

Perhaps the sentiment is more closely related to the quiet. If only people knew that. It's not the difference between what you can see. These concepts of good and evil, right and wrong have far more to do with what we hear, what we think, and what takes over our minds.

In the night, the burdens of our pasts berate us and remind us they exist without the noise and calamity of the daily ins and outs of society that distract us. The nights are quiet. When you choose a life like I have, all that surrounds me is silence and everything inside of me screams. It's a constant, just as it was in the cell.

Those thoughts that gather in the darkness for others are a constant for me.

All of the sins I've committed, the games I've played and the chess pieces I've skittered across the board only to have them fall ... the voices in my mind mull over each decision constantly.

Countless days have passed where I've wondered if I'd made a mistake. If the men I pit against one another deserved the fate I played a part in delivering.

Men have died and I've gambled on their lives in order to serve a different, greater purpose.

They've all been pawns and nothing more. The question of whether or not I'd made a mistake was easily answered with a name of a victim. Often dozens of them. All the little birds I couldn't save and occasionally, a bird I was able to help flee.

For every man whose downfall I played a part in, there was always a list of names to justify their deaths. The innocent and the undeserving. Each and every time.

As I step out of my car, there's only one name that echoes in my mind now: Delilah Jones. Her name is in response to my own and what justice I deserve. I cannot live if she does not make it out alive.

There's not a thing in this world I've held more conviction toward than that simple fact.

I played with her life and for that, she may already be dead.

With the bitter wind battering my back, I stare up at

the row of doors to these run-down hotel rooms. Delilah's sister pulls the coat tighter around herself and offers me a polite nod, as strangers often do. In my jeans and navy cotton sweater, with a phone held up to my ear, I'm sure she doesn't think anything of me standing outside the building, leaning against the fence. I'm just a man on a phone call going about my business.

Cadence doesn't know I was waiting for her to leave.

It's easy to return it as she smiles tightly and goes about her way to where she parked her car. I'm certain she feels the sting of the conversation she's just had with my brother as she picks up her pace. It's obvious she's been crying with her red-rimmed eyes and dark circles beneath them. She's a wreck not knowing where Delilah is and what's happened to her. Aren't we all?

There's a pain that resonates through me when I watch her wipe under her eyes with a steadying intake. One I haven't felt in so long. A pain that mixed with the smell of dampened straw as I lay freezing cold praying for either death or for the boy's scream to go away. I thought that pain had all but vanished, but the wound's reopened, rawer and more ragged than I remember.

Listening to the click of her heels fading in the distance as she goes, I recall Cadence's conversation with Cody. Not a damn bit of it was useful. It's unusual that the calls and meetings I listen to deliver next to nothing for me. Hours and hours I've listened to men debate and make decisions they have no right to establish.

This is the first time though I sat with bated breath, listening through the small camera embedded in Cody's briefcase, praying for some detail I've missed to unveil itself. Some bread crumb that would lead me back to Delilah. My throat is tight as the car door to her sister's vehicle opens and closes with a thud in the distance.

The only thing I've learned is that Cody sees people differently than I do. I once thought we saw the world the same way. A piece of me had come to the conclusion that we had a common understanding and mutual feelings about the world around us. For the longest time, that shared understanding offered me peace. A small bit of it, but knowing Cody and I felt the same way ... it kept me from breaking. He was like me. I was the constant internal screaming others fear at night, and he was the distraction and morals they feel comfortable focusing on in the day. We needed each other. It all made so much sense to me. It was perfection.

When it comes to Delilah, it's apparent we don't feel the same.

Cadence doesn't remind me at all of her sister. He's wrong about that, and the simple fact he commented that Cadence reminds him of Delilah is enraging.

There's nothing similar between them. Every nuance and detail, from their outward appearance to their character and their motivations, is strikingly different. The contrast couldn't be clearer. Perhaps they both heal others with acts of service, but one offers justice and the other a shoulder to cry on. Two very different things. I'm not interested in pacifying one's fears and past. The only thing I find similar is a slight accent that's worn off on our Delilah, but it was present years ago. She doesn't have it any longer; it fell from her lips long ago and never returned.

With a heavy inhale, the piercing cold fills my lungs and I take the steps two at a time. With every move forward, I go over the information I have regarding Delilah's abduction.

There was an organized team—quick, so more than likely experienced. The van was nondescript. The men who stole her from us were highly motivated. Which means the abduction wasn't solely for money. They weren't simply paid off; it's personal. Each and every one of them refused to spill a detail, sacrificing themselves rather than providing me with information. I offered mercy, but not a single one took up the offer.

All I needed was a name. Only one question needed to be answered: Who has Delilah Jones? A cold sweat spreads across the back of my neck as the reality taunts me once again. I've failed her.

Knock, knock, knock. Each pound of my fist is deliberate. In the past I've left a note behind for Walsh. I've never stayed. There isn't anything that could have come from us seeing eye to eye like this. It was only ever a message I wanted to deliver to my brother.

This message, however, he deserves to receive in person and with full clarity.

With my jaw firmly clenched and the sound of the lock unclicking, I wait for the door to open, but it doesn't.

It takes me a moment to realize he must've seen me in the peephole and decided to unlock the door and wait.

How long has it been since that very thought didn't spike fear through me? The last thing I've ever wanted is to be seen.

Turning the knob slowly, I gently push the door open to find the daylight scattered in stripes from the blinds and laying across my brother's figure. Motionless on the couch, he stares up at me. The sight of him disgusts me to the point that I nearly snarl.

In nothing but dark gray sweatpants, he's planted himself in the corner chair, a bottle of whiskey on the table and the glass in his hand.

He's nothing if not the image of a man who's given up. The shadow of stubble on his jaw nearly matches the darkness under his blue gaze.

"Contacts?" he questions with a horrid half smile that's undoubtedly forced. I take my time walking in and closing the door behind me. An air of despair lingers around my brother, the stench of it repugnant.

He's given up on her. He believes her to be dead. The

realization only spikes my anger that much more. "So a beard and contacts is what you do to go unrecognized," he comments as I take a seat across from him. I can imagine a different world, one where I looked just like him. Pathetic and distraught, and not at all ashamed to show it. I've never been so grateful to be the opposite of my brother. To be the one taken and shown what the real world was like.

He was the good and I was the bad, but together, we made the world a better place. Or so I thought.

"I had one of them," I say, commenting on the purpose of bothering to come here. "One of the men who took her." My throat goes tight and the air leaves my lungs in the single word *her*. I'll be damned if it doesn't hurt to speak of the recent events.

"And?" Hope drenches the single word and the leather chair groans as he leans forward in anticipation. I've no doubt he assumes I have the information we need. "What did he say?" he questions further, suddenly eager. Maybe he hasn't given up. I'm not sure why, but it makes the pain strike my chest violently. My back remains to him as I stare out of the window of this shitty cheap hotel room, knowing she stood in a room like this only days ago. Only sunsets ago she was here, and she was well. Maybe distraught and confused, but she was safe from what ails us.

With my head hanging lower, I stalk toward the end of the room and stare at the small fridge, envisioning the one in

Cody's loft instead. She closed her eyes for me and we shared our first kiss in that kitchen. I can still feel the warmth of her against my embrace.

Without an answer from me, my brother rises, his voice raised as he practically yells, "What did he say?"

"Nothing," I answer coldly, my mind refusing to move from where I know she once was. She was there for the taking, and I didn't do what I should have. I left her in the safety and comfort of my brother. I failed her, thinking that what they had would be better for her than what I could offer her. If only I could go back.

"Nothing?" The word sounds incredulous from my brother's mouth.

It only sends the irritation to skitter across my expression and the thoughts of what once was possible vanish. She's gone and I'm not the only one to blame.

My hand clenches at my side, so tight the skin turns white against my knuckles. With my eyes narrowed I confess, "He had a seizure before I could finish my interrogation."

Light dims from my brother's gaze, the anger he felt a moment ago vanishes and the same dejected look he wore when I first came in reigns once again.

The ice in the tumbler clinks as he falls back in his seat. He doesn't bother to wipe the spilled alcohol from his hand as he runs it down his face.

He's exhausted, as am I. But he's given in and that's

unacceptable. He's not the half of me I used to know.

"This is your fault." I spit the accusation at him. His gaze is nothing but daggers as he raises it to me. Venom lays between us, and the tension thickens from its bite.

"My fault?" He practically sneers the question.

"I should have known better than to leave her." I hesitate to say it, the words breaking something deep down inside of me and spilling a darkness I haven't let myself feel before. Jealousy mixes with the rage and disappointment as I add, "I should have known better than to leave her with you."

Cody's mouth parts, his bottom lip quivering with anger, but it's just as quickly shut, snapping and offering me nothing but silence. Turning his head to stare straight ahead, his eyes focused on the sofa as if someone lays there across from him, his eyes gloss over and he murmurs, "Fuck you." He doesn't move his gaze as he picks up the tumbler once again.

I can imagine what he sees, what holds his attention. The memories of her, lying on his sofa. He took her there once. All I did was watch as he held her.

I could have been the one to have her.

Instead neither of us do.

I'm reminded of my mantra and the reason why I left her with him. *Bad men always lose.* I was always going to lose her. It seemed justified to let him have her.

But he's just as corrupt as I am. They all are. The ones who find sanctuary in the day and the righteousness. All of us are bad men. It's just to what degree we share that piece of us.

This isn't how I pictured the reunion with my brother. My hands aren't wrapped around his throat, squeezing the life from him as he begs for mercy. He doesn't blame me as I imagined either.

A part of me knew he wouldn't beg, but I expected hatred in the same dose as I feel toward him. Some part of me still capable of feeling guilt and remorse is aware that he must blame me.

Perhaps it's because I feel it too. Whoever took her ... there's a very strong chance that it's because of one of us.

Just as the words I repeated over and over on the drive here are tasted on my lips, the accusations and spiteful truths, I'm silenced by his phone.

He's faster than I am, reaching for it as if doing so is enough to save her.

My pulse races as he furiously types back. I could look to see who it is and what was sent; instead I wait, unable to move. It's the fear, I know it is, that keeps me from breathing. It paralyzes me. Either it's something that will help find her, or it's nothing.

I would rather live in this moment of hope, but isn't that what fear is. You must be consumed with fear, to have even a glimmer of hope. It's been so long since I've felt such things pierce their talons through my flesh and bones.

"There's movement on Ross Brass."

It's an odd thing, hope. It flickers and leaves me with distrust.

Before I dare to question, Cody adds, "He's sending the information now." My brother anxiously taps his thumb against the side of his cell phone. He sways for a moment and at first I think it's the alcohol, but then I realize the fool hasn't slept in the least. I've lived off short hours scattered through the hours since I was eight years old, since I was trapped in that cell.

Instead of questioning his current sanity, I ask the more important question, "Who sent it? Is Brass the one who has her?" His name is one of several I'd put on my list of suspects. As far as I knew, though, he hadn't used his phones or credit cards. He has no associates in the vicinity. Facial recognition from the precinct hadn't pinned him or anyone else from my list in a ten-mile radius from Cadence's place.

Angered that he has a lead, our only lead, and I didn't know it first, I press for more. "Who's giving you this intel?"

My question brings his gaze to mine. "Evan, a member of my team. We've been keeping an eye on him since the threatening note that was left at her place." Herman's face shows clearly in my memory. Narrowing down a fine line of men, all threaded together with blue ink that connects their violent acts and greed, names appear in my mind. Lists of names. So many of them, but at the very top are Brass, Reynolds ... and Talvery. The crime boss who relies on

Reynolds for the laundering. The one who's unknowingly funded and backed the series of depraved transgressions. I fixate on a series of potential events, each one falling like dominoes. I move pieces and play out the game, but I can't focus. With every thump of my heart, her gorgeous face, her warm touch, and her perfect lips interrupt my thoughts.

Walsh and his partner type away. Messages coming and going as I wait, allowing myself to remember, allowing a warmth of memory to keep the hope burning inside. It's weakness, but that's exactly what she is to me.

"His movement puts him an hour away." Cody speaks up as he reads through whatever it is that Evan Aldaine sent him. "It's not his stomping ground."

"An hour in which direction?" I ask. "Which town?"

"Two towns over from her sister's. Saint Peters."

"Where was he seen?"

"Not him, an associate who was involved with the abductions before. He was at a liquor store when facial recognition got him. He used a pay phone around the back, and that number sent a message to an old device known to be used by Brass."

"She's only an hour away," I say, breathing out deep at the realization. Even if she's gone, she's close. "I need to find her."

Again the names and associations tally in my mind, I scour my thoughts and memories, but I need time and access to my information. Anxiousness scurries across my skin in a cold sweat. Time is ticking and time has never been an ally.

"When was—" I start to say, but he cuts me off before I can finish.

"Video surveillance from two hours ago." Two hours ... so much could have happened between then and now.

"So we have a name," I say and swallow thickly, trying not to think of what he's done to her. What *they've* done to her. If Brass has her ... it's revenge or silencing. Fuck. Fuck! Herman's death and all that blood is on my hands. There's not a doubt in my mind that Brass isn't aware I'm the one who killed him all because of that note. Because I reacted without thinking. He dared to threaten her, and I simply knocked his piece over on the board. I didn't think of the moves that would follow.

It's my fault. A chill runs down my back, but Cody continues. His heavy gaze blinking furiously as he rubs his eyes.

"That's all we have for now. Aldaine is looking into any addresses that any associates of Brass have in a twenty-mile radius of that liquor store." Cody leans forward, engrossed in the messages and reaching into his briefcase for the laptop.

A numbness pricks at my fingertips. It's because of me. My decision. I can barely swallow since my throat is so dry.

Another list of names comes to mind. Too many of them. The number of associates for Brass and Herman, and Talvery if he's also involved ... too many. "It will take hours." I'm not even aware I've spoken out loud until Cody responds.

"It's too long. Too many hours have passed already."

"We'll find them." Cody's confident in my moment of hopelessness and despair.

Whoever it is ... I will give them anything, kill anyone. I'll hand over myself in exchange. We just need to find her.

Chapter 5

Delilah

I'm going to die here.

After everything that's happened, this is how I'll spend my last breaths. It's hard to wrap my head around that fact, but for the last sleepless hours, it's all I've done. I've mourned the dreams I won't see come true. I've cried for my sister who's so very alone now, worried about both my mother and myself.

More than anything, I've pictured the two men I gave myself to last. My heart aches for what they'll go through. I've seen it before, written on the faces of loved ones. It's a pain that's undeniable when the uncertainty vanishes and the truth that their loved ones are dead can't be combated with hope. Especially for men like them. Heroes … or … whatever they truly are. Men of justice and power.

Even though I don't know what they think of my relationship with the other, I hope they both know I've loved them in the way that I'm able. Each of them. A hot tear slips down my cheek to my lips where the salt gathers and seeps into a cut there. Saying goodbye is what hurts the most. It's the last goodbye and I can't even do it with a kiss. I imagine it again and again, and each time the agony cuts deeper into my soul.

Evaluating the past is easier than thinking of what's to come. So many faces flash before my eyes. I don't remember all of their names, but their faces have never left me. As I roll over on the cold hard ground, staring up at the bright light they turned on full blast and left on, I allow myself to think I've made a difference.

For grieving families and poor souls who would have fallen victim to murderers, kidnappers and rapists I helped put behind bars. I've certainly made a difference in a few short years, but it's so very small compared to what I'd hoped.

One life changed is significant, I remind myself. Not a single thought, though, is enough to soothe the truth that brings me lower and lower: I'm going to die here. My hands tremble and I shove them under my legs, attempting to swallow although my throat is dry.

I don't want to die. My chest heaves in a breath as I tumble down a dark hole of despair.

"I'm not ready to die. I could have done so much more," I

whisper in a croaked voice and just like the last few times my thoughts wandered to what could have been, Marcus's face returns. His heady scent surrounds me, paired with the chill that's ever present whenever I think of him. Who would have thought the cold would be so comforting. If he could meet me there in my death, I'd accept it. I'll go willingly, if only he'll meet me there. My hand finds my cheek where he last held it and I imagine my hand is over his. I close my eyes, and I swear I can feel his lips against mine.

Creak, thump. The heavy door opens abruptly and the harsh sound rips through my thoughts. Swallowing down every emotion other than hate, I stare up at the hardened gaze from Brass. My body's stiff and anger flows through my veins, keeping my tired body from sagging.

"Brass," I say and his name is nearly a hiss from my lips. Contempt lengthens the single syllable. At first it's hard to see through my blurred vision, but as I steady my breathing, the red light that appears in his hand becomes more clear.

It also explains why his gaze isn't on me. It's on a tiny screen from a silver and black video camera.

Thump, thump, thump, my heart gallops away.

He's videotaping.

"I'm going to need you to do me a favor, Miss Jones," he says as fear creeps into the back of my mind.

Even though my stiff body turns cold from head to toe, I do everything I can not to show the terror that runs rampant at the thoughts of what he could possibly want to record.

As he steps in, so does another man. Slender in build, slightly taller. All in black and he wears a mask still. I'd feel a glimmer of hope at the sight of his mask if it weren't for the camera. It's not that he doesn't want me to see him; he doesn't want whoever is going to view this video to see who he is.

"My mother?" I ask him, needing an answer to one of the prevailing questions that have haunted me while he's been gone.

Brass tsks as the second man shuts the heavy door. I can't help but to watch as it closes completely with a heavy click and the slim light from the hall fades to nothing. Then there's another turn of a lock. Someone must've locked it from the outside. Or it's automatic when the door shuts.

"I'm so sorry to inform you, but," Brass begins and then takes a deep inhale as if it pains him to tell me, "your mother didn't make it."

My throat seems to close on its own. As if I'm choking, but there's nothing except for air present. The trembling that runs through my body is involuntary.

"Liar." I speak the single word while attempting to hold back the shock and grief. I prepared myself for that reality. I knew it was likely, but still I prayed ... Prayers have come easy while I've been caged by these four walls.

"We couldn't have any witnesses," he says and shrugs carelessly, although the thin, wicked smile stays put. "Your sister is lucky she—"

"Leave her alone." My statement was meant to hold a threat, but with the sorrow still wracking through my body, I'm only begging him.

"This is good, but this is not what the video is for, Delilah." Brass speaks clearly, not troubled at all as I heave in the wretched stench of the room.

My mother's dead. With my head spinning and my emotions swarming through me, Brass approaches far too quickly, reaching down with his left hand, the camera firmly in his right. His fist grips my hair close to my scalp and my neck snaps back as he forces me to stare up at him. The time is ticking away as I gasp and scream into the camera with its steady red light.

"We're making a family video, Delilah," Brass says. "I need you to tell Marcus that he wasn't supposed to intervene."

Marcus. His name alone is chilling. I'm struck from hearing it. What does he know of Marcus? My Marcus.

Another second passes, and it's too much time for Brass's liking. With a nod to the masked man, he releases me. Falling to my palms harshly, I barely catch myself, struggling with the pain from before as a fresh burst of agony rips through me. The masked man struck me so hard on my cheek, my head whips to the right, blinding my vision and I'm knocked onto my back.

It happened so fast, I can barely grasp what happened.

Marcus. What does he have to do with Brass?

"He took what was mine. He intervened and broke our deal." Brass's anger shines through as he answers the unspoken question. My chest rises and falls faster and faster as I listen to him, slowly piecing it all together. "Herman was essential and Marcus knew that."

Marcus did kill him. He killed him for me, and now ...

Crack! I scream out as my body doubles over and I clutch at my stomach. I didn't even see the kick coming. The pain radiates through me and I find myself huddled in as small of a figure as I can. It doesn't help me, though. Even as the cry is still tearing through me, the masked man fists my hair at the nape of my neck, pulling me up and forcing my bruised body to unfold as I stand.

"Now, Delilah, you need to tell Marcus not to intervene. Do you understand?"

Fresh tears leak from the corners of my eyes and I stare ahead at Brass. He's a man of confidence and so certain that he has the upper hand. I don't know what Marcus has done, but I know if I do what he says, Brass could kill me. He feels he needs me now. That in some way, I'm a piece, a pawn, in their game.

Even as my lips quake, I press them firmly together, barely able to shake my head from the grip the man still has on me. He yanks at me savagely, forcing a scream from me and shoving my body against the wall of brick.

"Say it!" Brass screams, eating up the distance between us. "Say it!" His scream is so loud and so close, it vibrates my chest, making it ache and the fear of what's next suffocates me.

Between every command is a beating. Merciless and unrelenting. I would stay silent if I could, but whimpers and screams are as constant as the commands.

"Tell him we had a deal."

Blood coats my mouth.

"Tell him it's his fault."

Betrayal and hurt are the only thoughts that distract from the pain.

Brass's next confession would hit me harder, if I hadn't already suspected it. "Did you think the evidence disappeared on its own?" Brass licks his lips, getting so close to me that I can smell the stale coffee on his breath. "Marcus is the one who let me out. He's the one who tainted the evidence. We had a deal," he says, emphasizing the last part with his brow creased. "He did this to you. You should loathe him."

Wincing, I expect another strike. Instead I'm released, watching Brass's back as he paces to the other side of the room.

"Say it." This time when he speaks, his voice is calm, gentle even. "Tell Marcus this is because of him."

I'm given a small moment to consider it all. Every moment that led to this before I respond, knowing I can't give him what he wants, regardless of my own conclusions.

"Our actions are our own." It's a truth I've said countless

times before. It's been followed by folders being slapped down on a steel table as I pulled the truth from criminals who committed atrocious deeds, but followed up confessions with *buts* and the names of others they blamed.

A huff that's half disbelief and half disgust is blown from Brass as he rounds me. His boots slap on the broken concrete ominously, but not a single piece of me stirs. I accept it. I will take what's to come now without hope of something more.

"I'm going to die here," I whisper out loud. At first it's as if Brass doesn't hear what I said, but slowly it dawns on him and a thin smile curls his lips up in the most sickening way.

"Yes, yes you are. And you deserve it."

Chapter 6

Marcus

I have to force myself to watch. Every whimper that's uttered from her lips, the quick and stuttered intakes of her breath, and the cries of pain she can't hold back no matter how hard she tries—all of it shreds me.

I tell myself not to look away, and it takes everything in me to stand perfectly still as I do. The projection screen fills the back wall of the hotel room. When the screen pauses, her eyes scrunched and her head ripped back by a man in a mask, I realize my blunt nails have dug into my skin to the point of drawing blood.

"The cell consists of four walls that have deteriorated. One of Brass's men was spotted in Saint Peters, and another has family only a mile away …" Riggins has a habit of thinking out loud. Once a young man hell-bent on justice, he grew to play a part of my Army. I was young and reckless when I had him kill his sister's ex. It was easy to do. I simply gave a boy a gun at the perfect time. That time happened to be right when his sister's ex was walking to his car parked in the back of an alley after his shift had ended. He would get away with it easily. I forgot, though … I forgot that killing someone, being the reason they've died, changes a man.

He was an innocent who tried to kill himself after he'd taken justice into his own hands. The attempt left a hole in his head, a scar on his face and turned him into a man who had no purpose. I needed to take care of him after destroying the life he once had. So I gave him a place in a world he could never leave. Charlie Riggins and so many others are my Army, and this is all they know.

The blue dry erase marker he's holding screeches as he sketches a triangle on the whiteboard. The computer screen he resides in doesn't have a camera on my end. I'm able to see him and anyone else I deem fit to be a part of this planning. For now, though, it's just us. "The map has three points and somewhere within this region, there's a bunker or a basement … something that's been added to over time, it looks like."

Riggins comments, "The additional stone appears to be the same as before. Could be historical."

"It could be the stone from a masonry." The thought leaves me, spoken aloud but not with conscious consent. My focus is solely on Delilah and the pain that etches across her face when Brass tells her that it's because of me he was released.

That's the moment she broke down. That pain that touched every inch of her being is felt inside me as well. Regret consumes me and I'd let it devour me if I didn't know she's still alive.

I can still save her and then I'll explain. I needed him for one more play. He was a pawn, but I made the mistake of not realizing she'd entered the game.

"Masonry ... one of ..." The sound of papers rustling comes through the speakers on the laptop as Riggins searches for something. The wheels to his desk chair roll him smoothly across the screen to a computer station. The rapid tapping of keys brings down the video of Delilah and replaces it with files upon files as Riggins searches for the connection.

My head hangs low and I can barely swallow the guilt that's thick on the back of my tongue.

"Someone's father or uncle. I remember seeing one of his associates has a masonry."

There's the connection. Reynolds and Brass are in this together and they'll die together.

"Bring up the video again." I give him the command but Riggins continues to guess, putting the pieces together the best way he knows how. I need to see her face. I need to see her again.

"Where did I see it ..." he muses as I struggle to keep

myself upright. "The factory maybe? And he's using the same three men who were in on the abduction of the girls." My frustration can't be seen as I lean against the desk to remain vertical. I let a man go who had three men in his back pocket with evidence to pin the case on. Three pedophiles and a partner who would back him financially, every step of the way.

"Could be ... if I recall, he specialized in headstones."

"They will all die," I whisper, my eyes barely parted, same as my lips, as I stare down where my hand grabs the edge of the cheap dresser.

"Yes. Reynolds. His in-laws own a masonry and at least two properties in the designated area."

A sense of control comes flooding back knowing we have addresses. "What are they?"

"One's a piece of land that looks to be about twenty acres in the middle of nowhere. The other is a morgue."

"Rewind it again," I say, standing upright to speak firmly. "Send the two addresses and rewind it one last time."

"Sir, we need to scan the vicinities—"

"Send me both addresses." My tone is sharp with the request and in return there's silence.

"Marcus said—" The fool still believes I'm only second-in-command to the enigma named Marcus. Riggins spends his days like any other coder for a private security firm hired out by the government. When I tell him Marcus is calling on him, he answers immediately. After all, he owes Marcus everything and Marcus has never told a soul what he did. He took the blame for the murder. He paid the hospital bills. Marcus took care of everything for Riggins. In return, he's asked for so very little.

The screen in front of me is stagnant as Riggins continues to resist. I'm only vaguely aware I'm on edge and not the calm mouthpiece I typically play.

Clearing my throat and ignoring the heat that surges through my body, I take control as I should ... As Marcus's second-in-command.

"I'm aware that Marcus wants every bit of information."

"That's what I'm here for, and you're rushing this." Riggins's tone holds a warning. "What we don't know is what will bury us. We don't move until we know." His dark gaze peers into the camera, staring at no one although I stare back. "You're the one who told me that. I gather everything we need. You execute the mission, picking the players we need. It's always worked that way. We shouldn't rush this."

I confess what I shouldn't. "We don't have time." The incessant ticking of the clock has tortured me every moment she's been gone. What am I supposed to do? Sleep, knowing she's being tortured? Eat, not knowing if she's starving to death?

"There is no reason to rush ..." Riggins's words are slow, his expression suspicious. He's a fool. He's a damned fool.

There's never been a moment in our collaboration where he's questioned me. He's been eager to have his rightful place delving into the darkness and aiding however he can. I was prepared at any point to kill him. He was going to die before I stepped in. Marcus saved his life, even if he's never realized I am Marcus.

"Sir ... I think you may be overreacting. Are you ..." His swallow is audible. I can practically see the wheels turning. "I think you may be ..."

"May be what? Distracted? Emotionally invested?" *As if I didn't already know.*

"There are two addresses. If you go to the first, and you're wrong, they could know we were there. They could prepare for us, and then what?"

"My contact and I will split the locations."

"We don't have men here. It will only be you."

His uncertainty and hesitation are infuriating. "Send me the addresses."

"You're not telling me something," he says, coming closer to the truth. "Does Marcus know?"

A sarcastic laugh leaves me in mourning. I risk confiding in him the longer this goes on.

"If she was yours," I nearly whisper, "if she was yours, would you wait any longer?"

Riggins's expression adjusts as the realization hits him. "This isn't about Brass and the cases." A sad smile picks up one side of my lips.

"No. It's not."

"Does Marcus know?" he questions again and I nod like a fool as if he can see me.

"Marcus is aware."

"Yes."

"I thought it was ..." he trails off and clears his throat. "Never mind."

"Tell me what you thought."

"You've slipped recently ... you haven't been focused, and I thought Marcus would notice and maybe he has ... maybe ..."

Tension rolls down my shoulders as heat burns its way through me, threatening and igniting a less forgiving side of me. "What do you intend to do about me slipping?"

With a click on the keyboard, Delilah's brought back in front of me.

"You should have told me, so I could step in." His voice is apologetic and I have to bite back my retort. He couldn't do an ounce of what I do. He's a hacker; he's a thief when needed, but he's not a murderer. He's not manipulative and decisive. There isn't a single other person who could take my place ... other than perhaps Walsh. Or so I once thought. He's the only man I considered being in a partnership with. Charlie and the Army of men I've gathered, men who owe me and owe it to themselves to join this fight are only pieces of the puzzle. They don't see the big picture. Not like Walsh and I did.

I stare at the paused image, her lovely face contorted with agony. Her caramel skin dirtied from both dry and fresh blood, and those amber eyes reflecting nothing but betrayal and sorrow.

The heavy thudding of my heart accompanies the film as it rewinds in front of me.

"I'll watch again while you send the addresses to both me and my contact, Walsh."

"Yes, sir," he answers dutifully.

It doesn't go unnoticed that, for a moment, I lost his unwavering support. For a moment there was a question and a hesitation. And more importantly, that one of my men knew I'd been distracted. If he noticed, there's not a doubt someone else has the same suspicions. That uncertainty adds to the fear that threatens to bury me alive.

Chapter 7

Delilah

SENIOR YEAR OF HIGH SCHOOL

I hear my mother before I see her. My gaze slips from my makeshift ponytail in my hand, to her reflection in my vanity mirror. With a laundry basket balanced on her hip, she shakes her head at the sight of me. "You're not going to the semifinals with that hair."

"It needs to be simple," I say in protest and look over my shoulder. My mom's happy today. Lighter than she's been recently. I think driving Cadence back to Auntie Susan's so she's closer to the winter gymnastics camp she goes to every year after holiday break upset my mom. It's like her mind's been occupied recently, and a dark cloud has been hanging over her head.

"It needs to be polished," she responds, taking the hairbrush from my hand and I have to bite my tongue. She's not wrong, and I've never been good at doing my hair like Cadence is.

"If your sister was here—" I can already hear her telling me how she'd have done my hair up like she has for these student government competitions the last two years.

"Then I could wear that blue jacket she had," I say, cutting off my mom and smirk at the thought. If having my sister at home was good for one thing, it was her closet.

My mother huffs and a smile forms on her face. I watch her as she brushes out my hair and makes it more presentable than I ever could.

"We should have gone to get our hair done yesterday," she comments, almost to herself I think, and her voice is forlorn. I almost tell her that I reminded her in the morning, but I keep my lips shut tight. She's having a good day, and I'm not going to ruin it.

"I'll do your hair and you bring home the trophy. How about that?" she says and smiles, pulling the hair tight with the band.

"It's not a trophy, it's a plaque and if we go to finals, a scholarship." I can't help the pride in my voice, but the nervousness shuffles its way through me too. The judges are heads of various university departments. I can't mess this up. My portfolio needs more accolades, and a scholarship couldn't hurt either.

"You're going to be so much more than I ever could." My

mother's musing breaks the silence. "I just know it."

"Mom, it's just a competition," I tell her, trying to downplay it. Dad said it's important, though. My extracurricular activities matter and first impressions last forever. Again, anxiousness wracks through me.

"I know, baby. I know." Her tone is ... upsetting. I can't shake this uneasiness as I watch my mother. She's so close to me, but I've never felt so distanced from her.

"Are you all right?"

"Just thinking about things, baby girl. Don't pay any attention to your mother." She puts the brush down on my vanity opting for a comb instead, and a jar of pomade.

"You're going to make this world a better place," she tells me.

"As if I need more pressure." I don't hide the sarcasm in my response. "You know you could still do something about making the world a better place."

"I already did. I had you and your sister."

The creak of the front door opening travels all the way up the stairs to my bedroom.

My mother peers at the open door, and I watch her smile fade and her movements falter.

"Dad's home early. Maybe he can come." I can't help but smile at that thought. He'll see me in action. My mother's smile reappears, mirroring my own but she doesn't answer me.

I can't die here. Not like this. Not yet.

Even though my body aches with every small movement, I push myself up onto my hands and knees. My palms press against the cracked cement floor as my body arches involuntarily from the pain of laying still for hours with so many cuts and bruises. I don't know how long it's been, only that it's been far too many hours of feeling hopeless and beat down.

There aren't any cameras in here that I can tell. The four walls of old brick could tell endless stories I'm sure, but unless I'm blind to them, there isn't a record of what's happened here apart from the camera Brass brought in. My eyes strain as I inspect each crevice again. Some stones are damp, others stained from water or blood or something else entirely, I'm not certain. Crawling and then slowly standing, I test any crack that may be weak from decay and time. Everything aches, but the pain doesn't affect me like it did before. It simply is.

I spend my time testing every weak spot, searching for any out. Nothing gives, though. The door is next. It's a foolish thought, but I test the doorknob. It's iron and the handle is antiquated. If I gave a damn about history beyond legal cases and precedents, maybe I'd know more about this location and what it was possibly used for, but I haven't a clue. In my wildest guess I imagine the Civil War and bunkers where men hid or held prisoners. The thought has occurred to me more than once: How many people have died here?

I question if I should risk screaming for help, but I'm

certain I'm being held underground. Given the damp smell and the layers of stone and dirt, I would be surprised if I wasn't hidden away beneath some rotten barn or perhaps it's only a small door, hidden in brush that would reveal a stairway and lead down to this dungeon.

I test the hinges on the door, praying they haven't been kept in good condition. They match the knob, so I imagine they're original. And just like the knob that's unmoving, so are the hinges.

Losing the last piece of hope and purpose, my arm drops heavily to my side.

I have no way out, no weapon. My mind races with all of the stories I've been told, the horrible nightmares that came true.

"There's always a way." I whisper the sentiment. I'm slow as I sit cross-legged facing the door. Someone will come through that door. That person, although a villain on the surface, will be my saving grace. He'll open the door and prove it can be done; he'll bring a weapon ... which I could take from him. Something, some shred of hope will be delivered with the creak of the door.

It's a soothing thought as I lay my head back against the hard brick and ignore the screams of pain from every inch of my body. My head is dizzy, my throat dry. I'm starving and I have no idea how long it's been since I was taken.

I told myself I wouldn't cry anymore, but damn if the tears don't spill easily while I wait for whatever it is to come.

Chapter 8

Marcus

Three days total have gone by since she's been taken.

Two hours have passed since the video was first sent via a link to an old burner phone that Charlie Riggins discovered. Without him, it would have taken far too many hours for me to discover the video had been sent. It was sent along with a threat but no demands: *You killed mine, I'll slowly kill yours and there's not a damn thing you can do about it.* Brass gets off on pain. He wants to torture me and he'll use her to do it.

I gave him no response. No threat, no reaction whatsoever. Anything I give him will only fuel his desire to get back at me by hurting her. What I want, though, is to slowly choke the life from him. To watch terror fill his eyes as I squeeze until the pumping of blood halts and his lank body goes limp. My fingers twitch at the possibility.

There are some men who are fueled by wealth and power, others by delivering consequences. Brass and I share this one thing in common: we're both men who fit into the latter category.

Too much time has passed and we have two locations. The addresses stare back at me like the wires to a bomb, one red and one black.

Riggins is right. If we go to the wrong location, we'll tip Brass off and he could flee before we get there. We could split up, but then we're even more outmanned and outgunned.

Fuck! There's no easy choice and we have to make a decision. Risk going to the wrong location and losing the element of surprise, or split up and risk being overrun. I slam my fist down on the cheap nightstand, and the particleboard splinters beneath the impact at the same time that my phone goes off.

I already know it's Walsh, asking me a question I don't have an answer to: *Which address do we take?*

Each second that ticks down on the clock is torturous as I scan the video for any other clues and come up empty. Delilah's cries for help drown me in those moments. She wouldn't need to cry out if I'd been there. If I'd protected her.

Once I decided I wanted her, I should have stolen her away.

I shouldn't have trusted my brother. I should never have let him lay a hand on her. She was always mine to have. And I belonged to her.

I haven't slept, I haven't eaten. I'm a shell of a man without her.

Staring at the phone, at Walsh's question I already knew was coming, I picture the two wires yet again. I can't risk the wrong choice, not when her life's on the line. There's never been a moment since I made the decision to be the person I am where I've felt such despair and uncertainty.

A moment passes without a response from me and Walsh calls, the phone ringing in my hand. Swallowing thickly, I answer it.

I don't know what to say, so I don't say a damn thing.

"You there?" he asks and at that I respond, "Yeah. I'm here."

"My partner is on his way. We can take the farthest address. Backup has been called. They'll be coming in from the south, so taking the northernmost option will cover our asses if she's at the south location. We'll call it in and they'll be there quicker than we can get there."

The very thought of men I don't know getting to Delilah first, risking they aren't corrupt and needing to have faith that they'll be able to save her ... I can't and won't risk it. I can't risk her simply being passed into the hands of another enemy.

"If you're going north, I'll take the south address."

"What? No, we can't split up."

"We can and we have to," I say, staring at the map Riggins laid out. He goes north while I take the south location. It's on us to save her. Not a man I don't know. She is everything to me, and who are they? They're no one I know or trust.

"I'm calling it in," he says, practically screaming on the end of the line as he stresses, "we need backup."

"I'm not waiting," I tell him.

"If they see you there—" The resentment that's lain dormant surfaces.

"I don't care." We cut both wires. That's my decision. It has to be done.

"Marcus. Don't be stupid. We need more men." My brother already sounds weak and defeated; I hate him for it. Almost as much as I hate the fact that Delilah loved him first.

"We don't have time!" How does he not get it? Brass only had her beaten the first time. The man is an amoral sadist with no boundaries he won't cross. Every minute is risking her. Risking further pain and suffering inflicted upon her and for what? For a better chance and better odds? I will save her. And my brother better be man enough to do the same. "Leave now. We don't have any more time to waste."

"Marcus ... Brother, please, don't do this." The sound of Cody swallowing is audible, fear and pain choking him. Was he always this weak? Or is he only weak for her? The question stirs up a pain we don't have time for. Hanging up, I leave the conversation where it is. He goes to the north address and I take the south.

CODY

Fucking hell. Marcus is going to ruin everything.

His impatience is unprecedented. "Pick up the fucking phone!" I scream into the line before pressing end and wishing I could slam it down to get out some of this anger. Tension rolls through my body, knowing I'm potentially headed to a hostage situation with only a pistol, no vest and Evan may or may not be there when I arrive. It's fucked.

With a long exhale, I try to calm myself as I take the next exit and find myself driving down a tunnel of overgrown trees. The canopy of branches above me simulate night on the dirt road lane although the sun hasn't quite set. I'm close to her and that's what matters.

Marcus will get her if she's there. He will. A part of me brings back childhood memories and times when we both thought superheroes existed. Back when we used to play Batman and Robin, when all was right in the world. Even then, my younger brother never did like playing the sidekick. He'd take off without me and do the things that frightened me without thinking twice. That's the man he is and I remind myself of that. I have Evan and the two of us have taken down far more dangerous targets. Backup is coming. If nothing else, we'll hold them off.

It'll work. It has to work. Marcus isn't wrong, we're coming up on seventy-two hours, Brass has to know he's shown his hand and we'll be coming for him. The stakes are higher now and time isn't on our side.

In a single text, Evan is informed and without hesitation, he agrees to meet me there.

It's strange that I would go back that far in my memory for such comfort, given the horrible deeds my brother has committed on his own for a decade now. He's murdered and slaughtered, he's wreaked havoc without thinking twice and all on his own.

He's never needed backup, he's never even needed me. If she's there, he'll kill them all and save her. And if she's not, then that's exactly what I'll do.

I'll kill them all. I'll hunt them down one by one until I have her safe in my arms.

My sweet Delilah; I'll save her.

One of the two of us will have her soon.

Marcus

The drive is silent and far too long. Even with the window down and the bitter cold air whipping across my face, I feel every second slipping by and it exacerbates my suffering. There are two of us and only one of us will find her. One of us will come face-to-face with Brass and have the pleasure of killing the fucker. My hands twist on the steering wheel, my thumbs running along the smooth surface of the leather. Death is not justice for men like him.

Taming the wild beast inside of me, I'm less concerned with him than I would be if she wasn't there. He is nothing and no one compared to her, and he has no idea of the depths I'd go to simply to know she's safe and out of harm's way.

I'm not certain if the locations Riggins sent are bomb shelters or something else, but Riggins sent the satellite images last taken from over a year ago. His search was unable to find more current intel. Assuming nothing's changed, there are doors that lead to underground tunnels hidden behind some brush. The radar showed several tunnels and each could have its own exit passage. It's a maze at best. A trap at worst. My phone hasn't stopped alerting me since I put the car in drive.

I don't answer; I won't negotiate with Cody. Even if we are outnumbered and outgunned, there is no excuse for failure. We have the element of surprise and the need to win. One on three or one on ten, it wouldn't matter. There's not an army that exists who could keep me from her.

If, however, we show our hand, arriving at the wrong location and tipping off Brass through security breaches, then there's no one to stop them from taking her somewhere else. Meaning it could be days or weeks before we have a chance to save her ... or never. He could kill her and walk away. We'd never have a chance to save her.

My throat is tight and my vision blurred as I hit the gas harder, revving the engine and tearing down an old dirt road. It takes another ten minutes before I have to slow and park alongside a thick row of pine trees. Beyond that is a small shed, decayed and rotted from years of unuse. I follow the map Riggins sent me, noting how the calls have stopped altogether.

Walsh must be there now.

Both of us at each location simultaneously.

Good, is my first thought, but then the anxiousness eats me alive as I take each step carefully, searching out the grouping of three trees that signal the location of the opening Riggins said was best. What if Walsh got there, and what if he doesn't have the same fight?

What if the worst of both outcomes has come true? The overgrown weeds hide the panel well, so well that I already know this entrance hasn't been used for at least a year. Tearing through it, I rip the door open, the rusty lock breaking easily.

The knowledge that it was far too easy makes one thing known—I cut the wrong wire. Even with that hopelessness washing over me, I continue the motions, wishing I'd listened and done what Walsh asked.

I contemplate messaging him, but I can't waste the time. It takes me five minutes to carefully make my way down the first passage. It's musty, dark and the light switches don't work. The wiring must be outdated and it's obvious no one's been down here for years.

Fuck!

My heavy breathing is the only thing that breaks up the silence as I make my way down the second passage, knowing damn well I sent Walsh to the other location and that's where she is.

She isn't here. I made the wrong choice. A cold sweat breaks out along my skin and I feel sick to my stomach.

There's no one here to fight, and I may have lost her forever.

Chapter 9

Cody

Everything feels heavy to the point that I'm reminded of both my immense exhaustion and the spot in my chest that pains with every small movement. The anxiousness running through every inch of me is so overwhelming, I nearly miss Evan's vehicle. It's tucked away behind the overgrown brush, camouflaged in varying shades of dark moss.

I barely glanced at the map Marcus sent, but I fucking hope we're close.

My keys jingle as I slam on the brakes to pull up close behind him, shaking off the fear of failure as I park. I'm quick to shut off the car and slam the door as I leave it; all the while my pulse thrums heavily and every movement appears to be automatic. Like I'm not the one doing it. It feels like I've lost control of my body, although I'm aware what's happening around me.

The truck rocks as I leave it there, meeting Evan halfway from his car to mine.

"Four men," he starts. The friend I've deceived thinks this is about a case that's gone wrong. The bit I fed him about a man who wants revenge is true enough, but he can't find out the details. My head's dizzy as I lean against the back of my pickup and look up at Evan, not sure how this will end for either of us. I'm vaguely aware at some point from this moment forward, Marcus and him may meet. That can't happen. I'm backed into a corner with no way out and everywhere I look, someone close to me is going to be hurt.

The deep bags under Evan's eyes match mine and I have to remember there's a chance this all goes according to plan. "It's just over there," he says and points, and it's then I see the binoculars hanging around his neck. "What have you got on you?" he asks and my response is a reflex, just like everything else.

"Just my Glock."

With a nod, he motions to the back of his sedan and I follow him, grabbing another handheld and a few magazines.

"I'll go in first and you cover me." I give the command, my jaw tense and the thrill of the hunt mixing into a deadly concoction with the fear that's consumed me. A darkness falls over my gaze as I stare off into the distance and Evan goes over the plan. If this were just like any other takedown, there'd be a hint of a smile on my expression.

But it's her. At that thought, the wind feels knocked out of me yet again. Evan's hand slaps down on my shoulder as if he can sense the change. "We'll be in and out, and she'll be all right," he says, his calm voice even and consoling. His brow rises as he waits for me to agree, staring back and not showing an ounce of nervousness. "She'll be in your arms in minutes and in your bed later tonight," he says, then lets out a huff of a laugh and it forces me to smile.

"Yeah." I nod and pretend it's all going to be all right.

The clouds ahead wash the entire sky in gray. The sun's setting soon and the dim lighting is on our side, but not so much that I'm certain we'll make it to the entrance without being seen.

"I'll go first," I say and nod, staring at the open field. I point to the trees where I can vaguely see a mound of dirt that stands out as if it doesn't belong. Before I can even question if he sees it too, Evan's already nodding his head.

"You'll need these," Evan adds, slipping a bolt cutter into my hands. "Anything else you can think of?" Without hesitation, I shift the cold metal tool into the back of the holster at my waist.

One deep breath and heat licks across my skin. Another and I silently give the motion, then the order to follow.

My pace is steady and my motions as stealthy as they can

be. I creep down to the field and hurry along the edge in the shadows until I come to the end of it. Pausing and waiting for Evan, I scan the perimeter, listening to the wildlife in the distance. It's a challenge, though, to hear a damn thing with the blood rushing in my ears.

A quick nod and another signal, then I sprint out to the mound, not covered by a damn thing and knowing full well Evan may cry out and bullets could fly.

Not a single noise ricochets in the air. Nothing at all as I remove the dried and dead brush, seeing the shiny metal lock and the two-by-two-foot panel that covers the opening. It's not dusty or covered in cobwebs, and that's a damn good sign they're still here.

My muscles are tensed and coiled as I hunch down and break the lock with the bolt cutters. A single groan leaves me, the sound carrying through the night along with the sharp crack of broken metal. My heart hammers as I wait a second and then another before pulling the metal loose and dropping it to the dirt with a soft thud. Standing higher, I motion over my shoulder, making eye contact with Evan and keeping a lookout over the horizon as he runs toward me.

Cold sweat lingers on my skin as he comes up behind me and I open the panel, my gun drawn and ready for anything, but all that awaits is a tight stairwell, aged and weathered from decades of uncontrolled heat and humidity.

I head down first and drop to my ass at the sound of a ping

as a bullet whips by and ricochets off the rusted metal wall.

Fuck!

Bang, bang, another gun fires and I push myself against the wall, firing back before I can even look.

Evan calls down as I search in the darkness and spot a man running around the right side of a dark and chilled tunnel.

He's dressed all in black but his figure is easy to make out as he takes off and I instinctively chase after him.

I can't lose him. He may be the only one who came looking with a sensor or security alarm of some sort alerting him. If we can get the rest of them by surprise, that's far more appealing than allowing this fucker to give them a heads-up.

"FBI," Evan calls out and I grit my teeth. There's not a word or warning that comes from me as I lift my gun and fire.

My first shot strikes his shoulder and as he falls forward, the man screaming, another person behind him stares back wide eyed from the other end of the dingy hall.

His expression is full of shock and I fire again, the handgun's grip sending a jolt to my palms as I pull the trigger again and again. Before the second man has a chance to react, I've shot him in the chest twice and the first man is silenced with another shot in his back.

"Walsh." Evan's voice comes from behind me and isn't the usual tone. There's a skepticism and I'm certain it's because I haven't followed protocol. I turn to face him, half-ashamed about my next move, half-eager to get it over with.

"Was he even armed?" he questions and I let my expression mirror his as it morphs from hardened determination to a look of disbelief. As he walks ahead of me to examine their bodies, I strike Evan in the back of the head, just behind his ear. The blow lands with a thud and a crack.

"Sorry," I mutter beneath my breath as he sinks to the ground. I catch him, the gun still hot in my hand and lower him down. It'll hurt like a bitch when he wakes up but he'll be fine in a day or two.

There were four perps on site; now there are two, and Marcus will be here once he realizes she's not there at the south location. Guilt seeps into my blood at the sight of Evan's limp body, but I can't have him witnessing what I'm about to do. There is no protocol to be followed, no honor in my actions when it comes to saving Delilah and delivering consequences to each and every one of these pricks who helped kidnap and terrorize her. I can't have Evan questioning, hesitating, or worse, trying to stop me. None of these men can be taken alive.

Evan's morals don't align with what must be done.

A door shutting catches my attention, lifting my head as I hear a familiar voice call out. It's unmistakably Ross Brass, and my gaze narrows as I stalk down the tunnel.

He yells for Mitchel, and as he does I gently kick the limp body, stalking past it and the pool of blood that's gathered around his chest, soaking into the concrete floor.

"Mitchel!" he cries out again, his voice louder, and the

adrenaline pumping in my veins pushes me forward. The layout of the tunnels is clear in my mind, and a plan forms but vanishes instantly when a second voice answers as I get to the *T* intersection at the end of the hall.

"There's been a breach," states a deep voice to my left. All the while I'm very aware of how Brass is positioned on my right. One man on either side of me, and only feet away judging by how loud their voices are.

"Fuck," Brass spits out. "Grab her," he practically hisses as the figure on my left suddenly appears in front of me, his gun aimed at me just as mine is aimed at him. He's tall, wearing all black and moves like he's ex-military—obviously trained for this kind of situation.

Just as I pull my trigger, two shots are fired from behind. *Fuck!* It could be backup, it could be Marcus. It could be someone aiming for me and now I'm surrounded. I don't have time to think. All I can do is fire away.

Bang! The man in front of me gets a shot off but he misses, the bullet passing to the right of me although it grazes my shoulder. A hiss is elicited from the burning contact, but I barely have time to feel a damn thing. Ignoring the pain, I fire again, landing a shot dead center in the man's forehead, and pivoting to shoot Brass in his back as the fucker tries to run down the hall. I should assume he's armed, but it doesn't appear that he is. His shoes slap against the concrete, once then twice as I pull the trigger again and again. A guttural cry falls on deaf ears.

I hadn't noticed my erratic breathing until I turn to face the dark figure behind me along the wall. Marcus. Relief is instant as I heave in a gulp of air. His sharp eyes meet mine and it's only then I'm able to take stock of what happened.

They're dead. It's over. But where is Delilah?

"How many?" Marcus questions and relief washes through me.

"That's all four," I answer him, searching down each hall for any sign of life, or any clues as to where she is.

He stalks toward me, slowly coming into view, asking, "Where is she?"

"I don't know." Heat races through my blood, mixed with fear at the thought that she's hidden and we'll never be able to find her.

"Delilah!" Marcus screams and it's the first time I've ever heard his voice so clearly. The first time fear has ever appeared in it. The same goes for desperation.

"Delilah," he cries out again and, in the distance, her voice is heard.

I shouldn't feel any bit of envy or the pang of regret, but my motions falter hearing her distressed voice, crying out for my brother.

He takes off toward her voice as I find a ring of keys in Brass's pocket. I nearly call out to him, but I don't. The words are swallowed back down in the darkness as I realize I want to be the one to unlock it.

Before I can fully stand, the clatter of men and the warning of "FBI, we're coming in," calls out from behind me. Marcus's sharp gaze meets mine from a distance and I toss the keys to him, calling over my shoulder and waiting for the silhouettes to appear.

"Down here!" My eyes drop to Evan's body and I yell, "Man down! Man down!" Footsteps and clicks of weapons being readied echo down the chamber.

"It's clear," I call out and then glance back down the hall. One man stays behind with Evan while another eats up the distance in long strides, his gun still drawn but held close by his hip. Two more follow him, each on high alert. "I believe she's down here," I say and motion with my chin in the direction Marcus took, before looking back over my shoulder to hear one of the men by Evan call for a medic. "I think I heard her down the right tunnel."

"Where's your radio?" the guy closest to me asks, his brow pinched. I hesitate to answer.

"I lost it ... I ... forgot it."

Shaking his head slightly, I ignore the questions that cloud his eyes. The ones I'll have to face about the lack of following protocol.

"This way." I give him the command but about halfway down the hall, I already know what I'll find. The door is open, the light shining a stripe across the freezing cold tunnel and it's far too quiet.

Opening the door wider, it creaks an eerie sound.

"She's not here," he tells me, and then calls out orders. The sound of the radio, followed by droning voices giving commands, all fades to white noise.

He took her.

As the men gather and split off to head down different tunnels, I already know they'll be long gone before the search is done. It all feels unreal as I pull out my phone, ignoring the orders of men superior to me.

It only takes ten minutes before the place is cleared. Five after that for my phone to ping while I'm fielding questions and watching my partner slowly being brought back to consciousness. It all blurs to nothing, the motions not determined by my conscience.

I stare down at my text: *Where are you?*

But more importantly, his response: *Nowhere you'll find us.*

"You weren't supposed to be there. What part of 'go home' didn't you understand?" my boss hisses on the other end of the phone. "How did you even get this information? It's not in our system."

I can barely pay attention to him as I meet Evan's gaze while his head is being bandaged at the back of the ambulance. The look in his eyes is telling.

"Skov is asking questions and I have to go into the precinct. I don't know what to tell them, Walsh. What did you get yourself into?"

I opt to hang up the phone rather than answer. The reality of it all slowly chills me to the marrow of my bones.

The look of contempt on Evan's face gives away everything he's thinking when I walk over to apologize. Although I still can't tell him everything. There's no way I ever could.

I don't have to guess what he'll say when I finally make my way to him, every consequence berating me one by one. "You need to tell me the truth, or I will tell them what happened."

Chapter 10

Marcus

She slept the entire three-hour drive back home. I didn't look back, I didn't listen to anything but the steady sound of her breathing and the hum of the engine.

With her in and out of consciousness, I cared for her how I've cared for myself too many damn times over the years. The makeshift ER in the basement is constantly restocked. These walls could tell endless stories about the faint scars of bullet wounds and broken bones that were mended in this room.

Riggins sent the doc, the only one I've ever trusted, who assured me none of her ribs were broken. The bruises that wrap along her torso send even more fury through me that Brass was given death so easily. I wish I'd been the one to take his life.

More than anything, she needed sleep. For fourteen hours, I watched her do nothing but rest while IVs gave her fluids and pain meds. She's badly beaten, but she's not broken. Not according to the doctor, but there's a different kind of brokenness that can go unseen.

A dark bruise rimmed with blue lines her jaw, trailing down her throat and it matches the other ones all over her body. I'm careful, with the sun setting on the second day, as I carry her to my bedroom, letting her rest in a more comfortable place. Slowly stripping away the dirty clothes reveals inch after inch of bruised flesh. Her perfectly caramel skin is tainted with shades of purple.

A whimper slips from her as her neck arches and pain strikes across her face when I pull the last piece, her bra, down her body. "I'm sorry," I whisper with every ounce of sincerity and I toss the bloodstained garment to the pile on the floor.

She's still in need of a deep sleep, but her eyes part just slightly and then she blinks, widening them and taking in a sudden breath.

"It's me," I say, then raise my hands in the air palms out to her. "It's just me, little mouse." I add every bit of comfort I can to my voice as she takes in the room, propped up on her palms with her slim body showing the sharp peaks of her collarbones. Every time I notice another detail of her abuse, anger rises from a simmer to a boil.

Swallowing thickly, I wait for her to look back at me, for

her frightened gaze to see me before I tell her, "It's only me, little mouse. I've got you."

"Marcus." She whispers my name and the dried cut on her lip cracks open. She winces and I leave her only to get Vaseline from the nightstand. The drawer opening and closing is the only sound filling the room as I carefully dab the balm on her lip.

She watches me and lets me care for her; all the while she's silent. There's a look in her amber eyes I've yet to see from her. I'm careful as I lift her in my arms. Her own wrap around my neck and I savor the feel of her hit skin against mine.

"Can you stand?"

She hums a quiet confirmation and I set her down on her bare feet toward the back of the shower. I haven't thought much of my home with its dated bones and barren features, but as I turn the white porcelain knob I consider explaining that it's safe. It may appear empty and abandoned, but this home is safe. Not a soul is around us for miles and the moment they cross that boundary, I know and the house goes into lockdown mode.

The hot water sprays down, just missing her bare legs as she presses herself against the wall.

It steams quickly and I can barely look at her, her nakedness against the white tile only serving to highlight every beating she took. Sickness stirs in my gut as I reach under the sink for a bar of soap. I lather the bar under the spray, noting she'll need the medical kit when she's done.

As I list in my mind everything else that she'll need, she reaches for the soap, taking it from me and turning away slightly.

"I can help," I say and she shakes her head at the offer, not looking me in the eye with her lips thinned and a grim look on her battered face.

I struggle to respond other than gathering a fresh towel and shirt from the cellar laundry. I waste no time, not sure what Delilah is thinking and with a million confessions warring to be spoken first.

As I lay the towel and shirt down on the sink for her when she's out, I don't hesitate to tell her the thought I've had for days now.

"I'll never forgive myself for letting this happen to you."

"You can't control what happens to me," she says and it's the first sentiment she's spoken clearly. Even over the steady stream of the water, I hear her clearly.

My lungs stop, my breath halting. There's an air about her that's unforgiving.

Control is all I have to offer her. I'm damn well aware of that just as much as she is. My gaze stays on the side of her face that's turned to me. It's unmarred and equally unemotional.

It's quiet for a long time as a new tension settles between us. I'm reminded of what Brass told her—the truth about my involvement in his case being dismissed. An ounce of suspicion or perhaps hatred has come between us; unanswered questions and accusations unvoiced.

"I said I won't forgive myself and I meant it." There's a coldness in my tone this time, a seriousness that's been absent since she's woken, but it doesn't faze her, although she turns from facing the faucet to look me in the eyes.

The hot room heats even further as the steam billows out past the simple clear curtain that barely covers half the space.

Without another word, she carries on washing her skin, stiffening when the soap glides over the worst of the bruises.

"You're angry with me," I start and heave in a breath, prepared to let her take it all out on me, but she cuts off my next statement with a simple no. She doesn't even bother to look back at me as fresh tears stream down her cheeks. It's the first time she lets the water hit her face and I'm all too aware it's so I don't see her crying.

"I didn't sleep while you were gone," I tell her. "I did everything I could to get to you as quickly as I could." The excuses crowd themselves at the back of my throat just as my hands ball at my sides into fists. Her stern look breaks down into agony at my words.

My poor little mouse. I've seen this look before. The pain, abandonment, the hate and denial. It fucking kills me to see her like this. Shut off to the world. I know it all too well. It's a look I've worn for years, but it's not for her.

Not for my Delilah.

"If I were to tell you that the idea of you falling asleep at night, not having the same confidence, the same fight, the same love and devotion you had before I came into your life ..."

"Stop it," she commands me and then both of her hands cover her face. The sob is barely heard but her shoulders quake with it.

Daring to continue, I watch every nuance of her response as I tell her, "If a night passes where you don't have those pieces of what make you the woman I fell for ... I would never forgive myself. If I were to say such a statement to you," I pause and swallow thickly before continuing, "would you try to let me in right now?"

"Please, I am not okay right now," she tells me, lowering her hands and staring straight ahead.

"I know. And I hate myself for it. I won't forgive myself—"

"Forgiveness." She bites out the word as if she hates it. "I'm certain you have many other things you don't forgive yourself for. Why should I be any different?"

Her question is a sharp knife to my heart.

"This is about—"

She doesn't give me time to finish before the accusation leaves her bruised lips. "You let him go."

"He was a pawn."

"He killed those kids."

"I know."

"You of all people," she starts but then stops, her nose scrunching as her body trembles. She reaches out quickly for the faucet and nearly topples over. I have to catch her and as much as she'd like to push me away, she doesn't have the strength. With the water spraying down my left side, soaking into my shirt and splashing across my face, I steady her and then turn off the water. She's lost weight, and this close to her, the darkness under her eyes is pitch black. Three days she stayed in a cell alone, beaten and left with nothing but the knowledge that she was there because of me.

"I'm sorry," I tell her. "I'm so fucking sorry."

"Why?" she questions in a pained whisper as more tears gather in her eyes. "Why did you do it?"

"Because there was someone else who needed to die. Because I thought I could play God." I answer her honestly as she falls into my arms, her wet hair soaking my shoulder.

It's been a long time since regret overcame every emotion I held. In this moment, it's all I can feel other than agonizing pain. "If I tell you I was wrong, if I tell you I would take it back, would you even believe me?"

She doesn't hesitate to answer yes, which offers me a slight sense of relief. I accept it greedily, I take the glimmer of hope that she'll forgive me and I gently pat her down, dressing her in a white T-shirt of mine when I'm done and bring her back to the bed.

Before she can drift off, I make her a bowl of soup. She's

only able to drink the broth, but it's something and she doesn't throw up from it.

With my back against the headboard, I rest next to her as she slips in and out of a light sleep. My head lays against the end of the iron rail and I stare up at the simple ceiling fan as it rotates. Her small hand, with cuts across her knuckles and her nails bitten back, lays across my chest. She placed it there the last time she woke, cuddling closer to me. It's a small reprieve from my ruminating.

Why did I do it?

Because I wanted to play God and I forgot ... gods aren't allowed to fall in love. I've never felt so weak as I do now. There's not a damn thing I want other than to feel her forgiveness slip into the cracks of my brokenness.

Carefully, I lay my hand on top of hers, just to make sure she's still here, still holding me, still alive and willing to lie here beside me.

The small movement and gentle touch rouse her and I instantly regret it. Selfish. I'll never not be selfish for her. "Sorry," I whisper and bring my arm around her small body as she huddles even closer to me. Every hour that's passed has allowed a bit of her wall to break. I pray time is on my side.

Her shoulders lift and the bed groans as she adjusts

herself. I barely breathe until she settles even closer to me and rests her head on my chest, allowing me to press my arm against her back and lay my hand on the dip of her waist.

I'll stay beside her for as long as she needs, mending every cut, tending to her every need until she's healed. I'll make damn sure there's not a single scar left on her soft skin when all is said and done. Not a memory of what they did to her will stay behind. Only this. The two of us, the way it should be. I close my eyes, comforted by the thought, but it doesn't last for long when she stirs.

"Why are you the way you are?" She whispers her question carefully and as I peer down at her, her lashes flutter and she stares straight ahead. Her thumb brushes gently along my side, making soothing circles.

"I found others like me, and that was enough." My memory drifts to what feels like a different lifetime. A small boy staring across a cell not unlike the one Delilah was just in. If she weren't settled across my chest, resting on top of me, I'd give in to the urge to move, to get up and do and think of anything else.

"I need more than that. I need you to tell me something. I need to know something about why you are the way you are."

"We can talk about anything else."

"Tell me ... tell me, Marcus." My name sounds foreign on her lips. There's a hesitation, a tone she hasn't taken before.

Sucking in a deep breath, I swallow the lump in my throat.

I hear his voice again as the back of my eyes prick.

"You already know, don't you?"

"You haven't told me," she whispers.

"You know I was taken, when I was a child. It happened so fast." My body's stiff but I heave in a deep breath, readjusting on the bed. "I was walking by myself to my aunt's house. She wasn't used to having kids. One minute there wasn't a worry in the world other than getting home before the streetlights turned on, and the next ..."

It's been a long time since I thought of that night, of the moments before I wound up in that cell. Delilah doesn't push for me to continue, but when I peer down at her, her gaze is fixed on the mirror, staring intently at our reflection in it.

"They kept us in a basement that was sectioned into cells. Four men."

"Us?" she questions.

"You've read the reports."

"They say you died," she whispers.

"Forensics weren't quite the same then," I admit, although my voice is tight.

"That doesn't explain why ..." she doesn't finish. It doesn't explain why I fled, why I didn't go back to my aunt's. Why I couldn't bear to trust or talk to anyone.

For a moment I contemplate telling her about her father, but it's far too risky when she's in a state like this and, more importantly, there's another person I've never spoken about.

Another soul who I failed and I'll never forgive myself for that.

"There was a boy with me. He was younger and he was," I stop to suck in a deep breath, steadying myself as I remember the details of what he looked like. "He had large eyes, the kind that are meant to tell stories," I explain. "He was my friend," I tell her. "For weeks we were in there and we had each other. Then one day they came."

I remember the sound of the gate opening, the loud creaking and how it startled me awake. "We slept together and when they came it woke us up, huddled in the farthest corner of the room."

"They took him?" she guesses and as I shake my head, I realize there are tears running down my face. "They grabbed me, but I got away and I went back to the corner." My words are careful as they come out one by one, afraid of being spoken, but more afraid of not getting out the reason why my soul is black. "I shoved him out of it," I say and my bottom lip quivers.

"We could see what they did on the other side of the hall. In the other cell where they kept all—" I can't finish and instead I remember how I shoved him out of the way to scurry to the corner. "I pushed him aside and he was closer to them."

"They came for me, and I sacrificed the younger, weaker boy to live a little longer.

"I watched, forced myself to watch when I realized what

I'd done. I'll never not hear his screams. He tried not to. He stared back at me and I know he didn't hold it against me, but they took their time and eventually both of us were crying. I swear I tried to convince them to stop and to take me. I begged them.

"They ignored me. They didn't stop until they were done. Raped him, abused him and after hours, killed him. All the while I watched and screamed for them to take me instead. That's the measure of who we are as people, isn't it? Our humanity. When it comes down to it, we'll sacrifice the ones we love just to stay alive."

"You were a child." Delilah's words are meant to console me as she lifts her chin, staring up at me, but I can't look back down at her. Not when there's more to say. To get out of me. I've never told a soul, but I'll give her my darkest secret. She can be a safe place for me and I'll be one for her.

"I was able to fight back. I didn't. I didn't fight and—" I almost say his name. It was so close to being spoken. "I didn't fight and he died because of it. Because of me. The next time they came, I fought and I got away. I killed two of them.

"I could have done it before, I could have fought and saved him. Instead I saved myself and this is what I'm left with. Memories of him trying to hold back the pain while they brutalized him. He held it back for me."

"His name was Marcus, wasn't it?"

There is no answer for her. Not one that I can give

right now.

I couldn't be who I was anymore. Not knowing what I'd done. I couldn't be ...

"I couldn't forgive myself for that. Everything I've done since then, I did for him. I did it because I was able to do something to stop the pain and injustice around me." My lungs still and refuse to fill as Delilah's lips part and stay that way, her next words unspoken and her bottom lip trembling. "But you ..."

The words are caught in my hoarse throat, making it feel as if there's a swelling that will surely suffocate me. A heat wraps itself around me, drowning me with an anxiousness I haven't felt in so long. It last held onto me, dragging me down to the depths of hell, when I ran as fast as I could. When my legs gave out and I had nowhere to hide.

It holds me captive now as she stares back at me, her amber gaze glistening with unshed tears to match the streaks of those that have already run down her bruised and broken cheeks.

"Christo—"

"Don't call me that!" I don't mean to lash out at her, but I do. I haven't gone by that name in over a decade.

It takes every ounce of my being to pry myself away from her gaze and leave at once. Forcing my limbs to move and ignoring Delilah as she calls out the name of the boy I allowed to be killed in my place.

The boy who comforted me when he needed it himself.

The boy who reminds me always, that the bad men always lose.

She cries out for him, for Marcus. Not Christopher, even though that's the name she knows I had back then. That's the name of a coward who chose not to fight. We could both be here if I'd had fought. If I hadn't tried to hide myself in a damp corner of a dingy cell.

I should have known better. I wish I could go back. I wish I could take it all back.

With the thud of my bare feet on the wooden floor, I ignore the tears running down my face as I leave her in the bedroom, locking the door behind me in case she gets the urge to follow, and take refuge in the empty room down the hall. I bury myself in the corner of a darkened room, huddled like I was in my most shameful moment and close my eyes. Wishing I could just go back and make it right. Wishing I'd died instead.

Marcus is the one who was supposed to live. Not me.

CHAPTER 11

MARCUS

"The cops are close."

Riggins's message on my phone causes every hair on the back of my neck to stand on end as I slice a peach, the blade of the knife traveling along the rough pit.

He continues as I watch on the monitor of the open laptop sitting on the worn laminate counter. "With Marcus the lead suspect in Mr. Jones's murder, they're digging into all the cold cases and overturned cases Delilah and Walsh have worked on over the years. Some of these cases are far too close."

I nearly question Riggins, *which cases?* But there's no point.

"We need to pin this on someone and make sure they stop digging. Pin every case Marcus has been involved in on

Delilah's father?"

"Marcus could be a disgruntled partner," Riggins suggests and every piece falls into place. It's the perfect plan to wrap up every loose end and fuck over those who have it coming to them.

"I know who can take the fall for it. I'll send you the steps."

Riggins asks a question he never has before: *How are you?*

Staring at him in the monitor, I know he's looking aimlessly into a lens I know doesn't show him a damn thing but a black screen.

"There are loose ends that need to be tied off. Let's focus on that." My tone isn't cold but regardless, Riggins's expression is less than pleasant. It appears he's reluctant to nod in agreement but he does.

Not wasting any time, I focus on the bastards who dared get between myself and Delilah and tell him, "All of Herman's team needs to be executed."

For the second time in the past few days, my ever-faithful companion objects. "Sir, if he's gone, then the connection to Talvery—"

"Do it." I leave no room for negotiation and reaffirm my position of superiority. "Someone else will fill the void and we'll nurture that connection. The next meet for Talvery's gun pickup is next week, isn't it?"

Although I already know the answer, Riggins confirms it and judging by his tone, he can guess what I have planned.

"Send Herman's crew to the same location. Let them clash over it."

Ripping the two halves of the ripe peach apart, I take my time slicing the delicate flesh, remembering how it all piled together. Every failure, every error I made that caused harm to bystanders like Riggins. I was able to help Charlie and bring him in close, but others felt the collateral damage of plays like the one I'm about to make. Mass murders of rivals meeting on trading grounds. There's a reason I have a reputation, and it's because I determine who lives and dies. There are so many bystanders, though: loved ones of those who will be taken from them forever and, like in this case, the unknowing individuals who do my bidding. The ones who were in the wrong place at the wrong time.

These are sacrifices that must be made, though. One beast will kill the other and if it's Herman's crew who survives, I'll find another way to end them. Either way, their days are numbered simply because they worked for the men who hurt Delilah. They'll all be buried ten feet deep before the winter is done with us.

"I am begging you to reconsider. They have ties that—"

"Every last one of them will die. Either by the supplier's crew or Talvery will end them when he discovers the mix-up."

"This doesn't solve the problem with the cops and—" Riggins's concern and hurried pleas are exasperating.

"I'll take care of pinning all that on someone who the cops

already suspect. It will clean up this mess."

"Someone they already suspect?" he questions.

"You don't need to concern yourself with it. I'll send it all over by the end of the day." I'm deliberately short with him, but before he ends the call, I add, "Thank you."

It's easy to see the small bit of gratitude in the slight lift of his smirk. "Any time, sir. Is there anything else?"

"You're certain it was only Brass and Herman who took her. No one else helped?" I ask again. It must be the third time I've asked in the past twenty-four hours. I'll question it a million times looking for someone to punish whenever I'm reminded of what happened to Delilah.

"It's confirmed. Yes. Only those who are dead, and those we're going to send to their execution."

"Very well," I comment and then end the call.

I finish preparing Delilah's breakfast and when I bring it to her, she's quiet but receptive. Silence is draped between us. After setting the plate down next to her, I sit on the other end of the bed, taking small pieces of the cut peach from her plate and watching her.

The questions are simple, both of our tones feigning a casualness that I sure as fuck don't feel: How do you feel? Did you sleep all right?

My skin blazes with both embarrassment from my confession last night and the vulnerability in this moment. I don't miss that when I look up at her, she steers her gaze in another direction and I'm doing the same.

She doesn't dare bring up what happened, but she certainly looks at me differently. It brings her touch back to me, though, the longing in her eyes and the absence of every defense she threw at me yesterday.

It's difficult to forgive an all-powerful god—or a devil, for that matter. It's far easier to have compassion for a mere mortal. For a damaged fuck like me.

Our fingers brush against one another when we both reach for a slice of fruit. Her simper is rewarded with a pleasant rumble I can't control. It comes from deep in my chest where it's still warm and safe for her. The insecurity of where we are now is irrelevant. It's like a dark room meant for safekeeping. A hiding place, perhaps.

I wonder if she has a place like that, somewhere inside of her, where she could store all of my secrets, all the hideousness and memories I wish I could walk away from and the stories I'd rather rewrite altogether. But in that same place, a little fire sparks when her hand brushes mine and she sees me smile. I wonder if that place exists for everyone, or if it's just something I have for her.

I'll hide all her secrets away in that safe place. For her and only her.

With those thoughts in mind, I take advantage of the easiness, leaning across the bed and carefully running my pointer under her chin to direct her lips to mine. She obeys without objection, her thick lashes falling as her eyes close. The kiss is gentle and I'm careful of the cut still on her lip, although it's healed slightly. The bruise on her jaw is still there as well. I'm cautious with every small touch, but not nearly in the same way I have been before.

With the warmth still lingering, I lean back, letting her chin go and watch as she opens her eyes and peers up at me with those gorgeous hues of amber. There's a fire there, one I recognize and thank fuck it's there at all. She knows my demons and my sins, but she also knows my pain and that's quite a different burden to carry.

CHAPTER 12

DELILAH

I don't recognize the person I am or the emotions that whirl inside of me, sinking to the pit of my stomach. I don't know what I dream of, but I know what I remember when I wake: the door to the cell opening, that click resonating, and then there he is.

Christopher Walsh, my dark knight, the grim reaper, standing in the dimly lit hall one moment, then his arms wrapped around me the next. He engulfs me, kissing my hair and telling me I'm safe, telling me they're all dead and they'll never hurt me again.

It's a moment of true terror, and then just as quickly, a moment filled with relief and love and a debt I can never repay. It's impossible to describe the crash of reality when I wake up, and he's hovering over me. Like if he dares to look away, I'd be lost to him forever.

The intensity of it all is at war with everything that's been embedded into my mind for days.

The simple fact that I was taken because of Marcus, is at war with the desperate need to lie in his embrace forever.

The battle is over with the whisper of a name each time: Christopher.

I can forgive Christopher easily. It's Marcus I have contempt for. Staring at my hero's sleeping form, I debate on doing something the logical side of me screams is mad. Still, the intention consumes me.

He has very few things in this old home. It must be from the '50s, a cookie-cutter cottage without any noteworthy or distinctive architectural details. It's lacking in maintenance as well as furniture. It's exactly the type of home I imagine the grim reaper would live in. A barren, cold and empty house. Last night when he left, I'm not proud to admit that I searched for a weapon.

I've seen grown men, victims of abuse, break down telling their stories. Only one I spoke with was ever violent, and shortly after he killed himself. Last night, Christopher reacted just as that man had. There's a sense of denial to it all, a fear of facing that reality before a quick draw of a curtain hides it all away and a different personality comes out to play. That's all it is, though, it's only a show.

He locked me in this room, and the same fear that washed over me watching a young man attack a social worker who was sitting next to me, hit me at full force. Mental illness comes in many shades. Christopher needs help. He's not well and that's a certainty.

I'm not well either, nor in a position to help him.

Still, last night I searched for a gun and instead I found cuffs. Maybe I am truly going mad, because as the soft sounds of Christopher's steady breathing comfort me, all I can think is that if I could cuff him to this iron headboard, I could talk to him. I could get through to him, I could rip back the curtain and help him in a way he so desperately needs.

For the last hour, it's all that's gone through my mind. The plan screams at me, begging me to do it. To slip the metal around his wrists and secure the other end to the iron rail.

I wouldn't dare broach the conversation with him unhinged. If he's secure, though, if he can't react and he's forced to listen, I think I could get through to him.

I could call him Christopher without him shutting me out, without him running away.

A deep sleep has taken him and all I've done is stare at his handsome form, noting how he appears so different. There's not an ounce of a threat and only a man lies in front of me. There's no sorrow, no pain. Not a hint of his troubles. If only I could see him like this when he's awake … if only I could see him smile.

With that thought in mind, I sneak out from under the covers, ever so slowly so I don't disturb him.

The floor groans, loudly snitching out my intention, but Christopher sleeps soundly. When I open the drawer, my back stiffens from the loud protest, but still, he sleeps.

I only second-guess myself for a moment, a very short one with the cuffs in my hand. He has at least four sets in that drawer and I have two, one in each hand.

I could cuff his wrists with one set each, and then quickly cuff the other ends to the iron rail.

The vision makes my heart race. I'm certain he would lash out if I don't do it quick enough. I nearly turn back, but a voice inside my head whispers, *Isn't that what he's doing already? He needs this.*

Without thinking twice, I don't attempt any careful steps. I'm not quiet in the least, and I'm not even gentle as I climb on the bed, linking one wrist and attaching it to the post before he's woken.

His wide eyes strike through me and force a yelp from my tight throat as I secure the other around his wrist successfully, but it's not attached to the bed. Falling backward I scream out, landing on my ass as Christopher rises, ripping his hand away, the iron and steel clashing.

"What the fuck are you doing?" he practically growls.

Anger and contempt stare back at me, followed by betrayal. My heart races with the fear, but watching him tug against the iron in an attempt to free himself calms me.

My caged beast is just that, caged.

"Cuff it to the headboard," I say, managing to get out the command in a calm voice, but it's so soft, he doesn't hear.

"What did you just say?" A threat laces his question. "What the hell are you doing, little mouse?" Rage seems to simmer around his shoulders. The moonlight shines in, creating shadows across his broad shoulders and sharp cheekbones. If we didn't have the history we do, I'd be terrified. As it is, I feel nothing but relief.

"Cuff the other end to the headboard." I give him the command and slowly stand. Only wearing a T-shirt of his, I rise and stand a few feet from him.

"You're going to run or y—"

"No." I don't wait for him to finish. "I'm not running." A deep crease settles between his brow and I'm thankful to see the anger wane.

"What are you doing, Delilah?" His question is still harsh and lowly spoken, but at least the fear is gone. That's what it was, not anger. It was fear.

It's been fear all along, hasn't it?

"I'm forcing you to stay with me tonight," I answer him and my fingers play at the hem of his shirt.

"You don't need cuffs for that," he counters. Instead of responding, I slip the shirt up my body and drop it to the floor, feeling my hair cascade down my bare back.

"Cuff," I say, whispering the single word. Vulnerability and a hint of fear that this won't work make themselves known, but mostly desire takes over. The heat in his eyes intensifies as his gaze travels the length of my body.

A moment passes and all I can hear is my breathing pick up. He seems to question me, glancing between the cuff and then my naked body.

"You better not lie to me," he warns and I offer him a sad smile.

"No lies."

When the cuff clinks and locks around the headboard, I tell him to lie down.

"Since when do you give the commands?" he asks, but does as I say. Positioning himself on the bed in a sitting position, he then slowly lowers himself so he's lying down.

"Lower still, so your arms are—"

"No," he cuts me off and there's a hint of defensiveness. It doesn't escape me that he could cover himself in a way as he is now. Although his hands are cuffed, he could easily kick out or fight in some capacity.

I could fight him on this, but I don't. I don't want to fight him at all and he's already given me what I asked.

I'm silent as I climb onto the bed, and each time I look up at him, he's staring at me with an intensity that's indescribable. It's like the prey daring the hunter. Power and lust are a deadly cocktail and they're all I can taste as I crawl toward him and tug his pants down his body. He helps me, lifting his hips, but both of us stay silent. The heater kicks on and the cuffs clank against the iron; other than that, it's only the blood rushing in my ears that I can hear.

His cock is already stiff, standing upright and waiting for me. My heart hammers as I wrap my hand around his length. With my eyes on his, I press my lips to his head and lick the bead of precum. I hadn't planned this, but I can't deny that it eases the tension. More than anything, I want him.

With my tongue starting at the bottom of his shaft, I lick up to his head, loving the rough hum of satisfaction he gives me. Holding him steady at his base, I swallow him down as much as I can while pressing him to the back of my throat and moaning.

"Fuck." Christopher murmurs the sexiest groan I've ever heard, his heels digging into the bed and his hips thrusting up.

The cuffs clink as he pulls against them again and they get my attention. I'm already hot, desire and the slight chill in the air pebbling my nipples. Without hesitation, I spread my legs and climb on top of him, sitting around his hips. I don't dare push him inside me, though, not yet.

"I told you, you would beg me," Christopher states, his lips staying parted with his heavy breathing matching my own. "I didn't expect you to steal that pleasure from me."

"I could still beg you," I answer and then drop a kiss onto his chest. My hair falls around my shoulders, landing on his broad chest as I plant kisses there and trail up to his neck. My clit presses against his pubic hair and the sensation overrides my common sense. As the heat builds inside of me, I rock against him, taking pleasure in the small motions, kissing and sucking up his neck, the rough stubble leaving small scratches behind, but I don't care.

When my lips meet his, he leans forward to deepen our kiss, his tongue pressing against my seam until I grant him entry. Although I'm on top, although he's the one bound, the kiss is very much led by him, possessive and demanding.

And I love it.

It takes everything I have in me to break it, letting my forehead rest on his as I whisper against his lips, "You lied to me."

I'm all too aware that his body has stiffened and I know his eyes are open with his lashes brushing against my face, but I keep mine closed.

"I didn't," he says and his response is whispered against my throat.

My swallow is audible, the fear of confrontation rising, when I answer him, "You told me your name was Marcus."

A prickling sensation travels down my body, as cold as ice and I don't dare move, much less open my eyes as he sits up higher, jostling my body as he does.

"I am many things, but I'm not a liar. You knew me as Marcus and that's who I am."

Slowly I open my eyes, kissing his lips that don't move.

"Tell me what your name is." I give the command, but I'm begging him and he knows it.

"Stop it." His own inhale stutters and my heart breaks for him.

"Please," I beg.

There's a heat and intensity between us that is raw and fragile, so easily broken but that's why it's so precious.

"Your name is Christopher."

"Stop it." His whisper is just as much a plea as my own and tears gather in my eyes as I confess, "And I love you. I love you and I'm so sorry for what happened to you."

"Don't say that name ever again," he warns me, but he doesn't move. He could buck me off, he could push me to the side with his body. He could fight back still, but he doesn't. He doesn't move in the least.

Not until I remind him, "You're the one who's cuffed, Christopher."

In a swift movement, he whips his body around, his arms crossing above my head as I'm thrown under him with a loud yelp.

Naked and caged beneath him, I nearly kick out, my legs drawing forward, but I spread them instead so I don't hurt him. With his hips between my thighs, my back pushed into the mattress, his rigid cock presses against my heat.

The shadows dance along his strong body as he hovers

over me.

"Stop it," he warns and I shake my head, even now as I've lost my position that only held a semblance of power.

"I love you, Christopher."

There is anger and pain etched into the chiseled features of his face as I lie there under him, daring to reach up and cup his chin. Although he stares down at me, giving commands and taking away my power, it doesn't stop me from kissing him and he kisses me back. At first he merely molds his lips to mine, and then soon he's kissing me deep, feverishly taking from me.

Reaching lower, I guide him inside of me and then kiss his throat. I tilt my hips up as he thrusts his down, stilling inside of me when I gasp.

His girth stretches me to the slight point of pain, but the pleasure is so overwhelming the pain doesn't matter. It only adds to my desire for more.

He's still cuffed and it makes it harder for him until I slip under him, down the bed and let his forearms rest beside me.

The moment I kiss him and tell him I love him again, he fucks me ruthlessly. It's a punishing fuck and I bury my screams in the crook of his neck, the smothering heat and overwhelming pleasure rocking through my body.

CHAPTER 13

CODY

"Where is she?"

"I don't know," I say and my answer is riddled with the irritated energy I've had all night with him.

"You mean to tell me—"

"That I arrived. I heard her. I had to defend myself and by the time you got there, my partner was unconscious and she was gone. Yes," I snidely hiss the last word, my hackles raising as my palms dig into the steel table I lean across. "Yes, Detective Skov, that's what I'm telling you and I fucking hate you for it." I let it all out, the pain and frustration and disgust at how she slipped through my fingers and ... how my brother stole her from me. "I loathe your sorry ass, and I hope you go to bed every goddamn night knowing she's still missing because of you."

His dark eyes narrow into thin slits as he bites back for me to watch it.

"Fuck you," I bellow from deep in my chest. The only thing that keeps me from striking out at him, is the very firm fact that every bit of what I've told to him, I've condemned myself for as well. "I fucking hate you and the fact that you let her get away."

"Let her? Did she just up and walk away then?"

"Fuck you," I manage to repeat as I fall back into the metal chair.

"Did she run away from you?" Anger blisters from every part of me as my fist clenches in response. The door to the room that's become my second fucking home slams open.

"Enough," Skov's partner, Gallinger, barks. His slim frame appears even lankier with a cleanly shaven jaw. He slaps a folder down, this one thin and pulls back the other chair to take a seat facing me across the table. Skov is silent, but his shoulders tense. Whatever Gallinger has, it pisses Skov off which should give me comfort, but not a damn thing can soothe the pain that's run through me since I searched that cell and saw she was gone.

She left with him. I went through hell to get to her, and I didn't even get to see her to know she's safe.

"What do you know of Delilah's father?"

My gaze rises slowly to his. "Never met him."

"What about the cases he worked on," he says, then shifts his weight from left to right. It's a nervous energy I haven't seen from Gallinger yet.

"What about his cases?" I question and then shake my head. "He hadn't been on a case in … decades."

Silence sits between us.

"He was murdered," the detective starts and I keep my expression as neutral as possible. I can't give a damn thing away. Aiding and abetting is not on the list of crimes I intend to go down for.

"The evidence points to a partner."

"A partner?"

The folder opens slowly, at the same time that Skov uncrosses his arms. Pictures appear of a young woman in black and white, and then another.

"A partner who had an appetite for young women and then went younger."

"Brass and Jones?" I'm flabbergasted.

"It explains a number of things but more than that, there was evidence found in Brass's home. Trinkets and keepsakes of the women. Things related to other cases."

"What does that have to do with Delilah's father?"

"He kept photographs. We suspected him …" Gallinger trails off as he shares a glance with Skov. "But not to this extent, and there was no evidence of a partner."

"You're shitting me," I say, feeling my shoulders stiffen.

"There's no way her father—"

"He was nearly disbarred several times over the years for a series of claims. The women dropped the charges, but a pattern is a pattern and the timeline makes sense.

"We'll ask again, what do you know of Delilah's father?"

"Not a damn thing," I reply without hesitation. I'm struck by disbelief, so much so, it takes me longer than it should to add, "I don't have anything to say. So either let me go, or I want my lawyer."

The air turns colder as the two men sit back in their seats.

"If you've got your suspects—" I start to say but Skov interrupts.

"They're both dead and your girlfriend is still missing. It's convenient, don't you think?"

Leaning forward, I keep the threat in my voice thinly veiled as the command is murmured darkly, "Keep her out of this." My heart hammers and I can't breathe until the chill settles between us.

"You're free to go, Special Agent Walsh ... from this interrogation, although I've heard your superiors are wanting explanations. Apparently there are some things that don't add up in your story."

"What about Delilah?" My throat is tight. I'll be damned if I let them stop looking for her. Marcus is a selfish prick and I don't trust him to give her back. I don't trust him at all anymore. I don't trust anyone.

"Her sister heard from her. She's no longer a missing person."

My eyes widen and I stare between the two of them as Gallinger closes the folder.

"You look shocked, Special Agent Walsh." Skov is nearly cocky with his comment.

Biting my tongue, I let the fact that she's safe outweigh the hurt of knowing my phone hasn't gone off. She didn't reach out to me. Neither of them did.

"You're lucky Evan Aldaine doesn't remember what happened to him," Skov says as he rises from his seat, indicating this interrogation is over.

"How's that?" I question, not bothering to look up at him as a prick travels down the nape of my neck. I stay in my seat although the two men are standing and the door to the interrogation room remains wide open.

"My guess is that you went in to save her from shit you caused. He went with you as your backup but you couldn't let him see whatever it was you did."

The shit I caused ... his assumption hits far too close to home.

"Maybe it's because you went in with the intent to kill those perps," he says and shrugs, in the nonchalant way that he has to make it seem as if the most horrid things don't concern him, "I can't blame you for that." Sucking air between his teeth, he adds, "I'd have killed them too.

"But my guess is that she didn't want you to save her, did she?" His question gets a huff from me as I stare straight ahead, ignoring both of their gazes that penetrate the most vulnerable parts of who I am. "She ran away, didn't she? She knew this all happened because of you."

"If it happened because of me, then how is it that her father was involved with Brass and coincidentally died just a week ago?" I dare to question him, finally meeting his gaze.

"Why don't you tell me?" he prods, lifting a brow.

It's easy enough to smirk at him and respond, "Why don't you go fuck yourself?"

"The only reason I'm not worried about your ex, and I'm taking a leap there, I know. I just assume she's your ex now ..." his comment is meant to get to me, and it fucking does but I do my best not to show it, "... is because you aren't yelling at us to find her. You know damn well she left you."

Insecurity grips me at the back of my neck.

"You're free to go, Walsh. If you have any information for us ... be sure to drop by." Skov's condescension is laid on thick.

Gathering my things, I head out, hating this place. Hating every fucking thing. Shrugging my leather jacket on, I turn right to head to the parking lot and get the hell out of here. With my phone in my hand, I nearly miss Evan standing to the right of the building, a cigarette in his hand, the end of it glowing bright burgundy and smoke billowing from his mouth.

Fuck.

"Evan." Shame keeps me from holding his gaze. Fog forms in front of my face. The temperature is only going to drop further tonight with the storm coming in. Rain washed away the snow, but what comes tonight will stick.

"I thought about calling and leaving this in a message, but then I thought maybe I could tell if you're lying to me better in person." Evan's statement is a slap to my face and I deserve it.

He doesn't owe me a damn thing after what I did to him. If I'd failed and that fucker killed me ... he'd have killed Evan next.

"I'm sorry." I say words that I know don't fix a damn thing.

Blowing out the smoke, he drops his cigarette to the pavement, stubbing it out with the heel of his sneaker.

"You need to go into the office—don't tell them anything other than you want to resign." There's not an ounce of emotion in his tone, only an order spoken dispassionately.

"What?"

His gaze narrows for a moment, but then it's gone. There's no animosity, only certainty that stares back at me. "It is what it is, Walsh. You stepped out of line. We've known for ... how long now?"

"I don't know what—"

It's surprising how grateful I am that he silences my lies. "If you don't resign, they'll keep looking into it. From what I can tell, you brought that lawyer into it. You want her to go down too? End it."

"I'm sorry."

"You used me. For a woman." Contempt finally shows up to the conversation.

At least I have the balls to own up to that. "I did."

"Don't ever come to me for anything again." He holds my gaze as he adds, "You're dead to me."

My throat is tight with remorse. "Evan, I—" The knowledge that I betrayed him in the most heinous of ways keeps me from continuing.

"What is it, Walsh? Spit it out."

"I fucked up and if I could go back, I'd change it."

"Was it worth it?"

I hesitate, letting the question sink in. Which part? All the way back to the beginning? *Was it worth it?* Were all the lies and deceit, all the murders and corruption worth having my brother in my life? Was it worth it to deliver justice to those who would have gotten away with creating more pain and misfortune than they already had? Was it worth it to fall in love with a woman who could never love me back? Was it worth it?

I can't answer the question. The silence lasts too long between us. A look of disbelief accompanies a huff of disgust from Evan as he looks past me, shaking his head.

"Don't call me again." Before I can respond he adds, giving me nothing but his back as he walks away, "I told our boss to expect your letter of resignation on Monday."

Chapter 14

Marcus

With her in the bathroom, I'm quick to sit up on my knees, press my shoulder against the headboard, and push on the top rail. It's old and the metal gives against my strength. Gritting my teeth, I have to heave my weight against it once more to slip the thin cuffs up the column.

I'm quiet while I consider my next steps. Silently stalking to the dresser, I take a moment to unlock the cuffs from my wrists and the other ends that were attached to the iron rail.

She is strong; she is determined. And that does nothing but make me hard for her. However, I have my limits and my little mouse is going to learn she can't take advantage of me in any capacity and get away with it. With the cuffs free I make my way back to the bed, right where I was. The water at the sink turns off as I slip the two cuffs around the pole that isn't attached to the broken rail. This one won't give like the other did, not with Delilah's small frame.

Lying down with my hands above my head, I wait for her. I'll wait as long as I have to in order to get her in my place instead.

Christopher. She dared bring up that name. The only thing that keeps me sane is her desire to love me with her words and her body. When she leaves the bathroom in all her nakedness with the pads of her feet against the bare floor, I focus on that. On her desire to use that strength she has, to try to heal me. To love me.

I'm already hard again for her and filled with the thrill of teaching her a lesson.

There's not a bit of her that has any suspicion as she lies down right where she was before, content on falling back to sleep, I imagine. With her head on the pillow, her body close to mine and one hand on my chest, I know it's going to be difficult to get both of her wrists cuffed to the bed. I decide I'll take them one by one. The first is the crucial one. If I can get one with hardly any fight from her, I can force the other. My heart pounds in my chest. She brought this upon herself. And I love it.

I love that she has fight in her.

Making my moves as quick as I can, I snatch her hand from my chest and pull it to the cuff. It slips around her wrist as her eyes go wide.

She struggles with a yelp and a violent push against my chest, but I'm faster. I'm stronger, and it's easy to pin her down and close the cuffs around her wrist.

"No!" she finally yells out.

"Oh no, little mouse, you started this game."

Her body writhes against mine, her gasps undeniably filled with fear. The cuffs click as I link them together, placing her thin frame where she held me captive. The heat of her body is addictive, her curves against mine everything I've dreamed of for years. As my fingers trail down her soft skin, and the goosebumps travel along with my touch, she begs me to stop.

To stop.

My body's still pressed against her as tremors run through her. For a moment, I worry I've hurt her; I lift my weight and account for every bruise. Even still she violently pulls away from the cuffs, with motions that do nothing but dig the metal deeper into her wrists. A moment passes, followed by another before I realize what the two of us were thinking are two very different things.

Her amber eyes don't peer into mine with pupils dilated from desire. Instead they're closed tight with fear etched onto her features. I hate myself.

A sudden gasp warns me of the silent sob that threatens to spill from the only lips I've ever craved to kiss. With the tips of my fingers just slightly brushing up her tank top, I wait for her to calm down. I let a moment pass as the seconds tick by, praying she'll come to her senses.

But I'm the one who's confronted by the hard reality with every breath that passes and the panic not leaving her stiff body. She's terrified of me.

"I would never hurt you," I murmur and I'm not sure she heard me as tears leak from the corner of her eyes and her face presses against the pillow, refusing to meet my gaze. Clearing my throat, I tell her again, clearer and louder, "I'm not going to hurt you."

My timbre trembles toward the end of my statement and that's when I truly realize the damage of this raw moment between us. Both of us bared, and both of us scarred.

"You think I'd hurt you?" My tone is wounded.

Delilah's inhale is stuttered with tears caught in her thick lashes. Bruises still linger along her cheek and down her jaw. I'm gentle as I cup her face, mindful of the pain she's in. I swear I can feel it, I can feel her pain, and I haven't the faintest idea if she can feel mine.

My gentle touch only elicits a harsh whimper from her. With my throat tight and the haze of what I thought was between us subsiding, I lean back, listening to the bed groan as I put more distance between us.

Instantly her nipples harden, the cool air replacing my warmth and I climb off the bed, placing the comforter over her body. With her wrists bound to the headboard, just as she'd cuffed me, I wait for her to look at me. Her lips are cracked and her eyes puffy. Her body badly beaten and weakened. Yet she's still perfect to me.

When her sobs cease and she dares to peek up at me, I repeat the sentiment, "I would never hurt you."

Shame seems to wash over her, but she doesn't respond. She doesn't tell me that she knows I wouldn't. It's a sharp knife to my heart realizing that she doesn't know that truth. How could she not know?

"I thought you loved me," I tell her and instantly feel foolish at the confession. Maybe it was something else. *Pity.* It's been so long since I've fallen victim to that emotion. She didn't love me, it was only pity.

"I do." My gaze whips up from my battered hands to hers. The room is dark, the blinds and curtains still closed tight. It's so quiet I can hear her swallow. "I do love you," she admits, and I swear my heart pumps once, sending the warm blood where it's meant to go, but it's far too slow to keep the organ beating. There's too much pain that floods the space.

"You thought I was going to hurt you," I say, stepping back and the floorboard creaks beneath my weight. That's when I realize I've never allowed anyone in here. There isn't a soul who's entered my home since the day I claimed it.

Yet I brought her in here, because, for some absurd reason, I thought she belonged here. It didn't occur to me that perhaps I shouldn't have brought her here. Not until this moment, as she stares back at me. Her eyes are filled with a knowing look as she whispers, "Yes, you scare me."

The confession forces me to turn my back to her, my palms keeping me steady and upright as I flatten them against the top of the dresser. The old wood feels cold beneath my skin, but it holds me up as I let it sink in.

"Christopher," she calls out and instinctually I condemn the name with a threatening tone as I tell her, "Don't say that name again." The murmur awards me a sharp intake from behind me. Yet again, since I've taken control, I hate myself.

Loving her has proven that in spades. The more I love her, the more I hate myself. Every event leading up to this moment swarms me. Regret lingers on all of them.

I question everything. Even the moments in the barn, when I let her father live because he truly loved her. How ... wrong. How fucked up! Anger simmers along my skin and I rip away the thin T-shirt. My blunt nails drag across the back of my shoulders and up the nape of my neck.

"You scare me, but I love you."

"Don't lie to me," I bite out, leaning forward on the dresser and slowly opening my eyes to see my reflection as I add, "I don't deserve that." The moment the statement is spoken, I deny it; I deserve everything she throws at me. I don't hold any right to anything from her. Certainly not her honesty when I've kept so much from her for years. Sorrow and regret chill my skin, to my flesh, down to the marrow of my bones.

She murmurs, "You can love someone while fearing them."

"No, you can't." It hurts to admit that, especially to her. To the only person I know I've truly loved since I was a child. Maybe I'm broken inside, so badly broken that I can't recognize what true love is. I only imagined it.

No, that's not true. Denying the question in my head, I know damn well I love her. I have loved her for as long as I can remember now. Hanging my head, I mutter, more to myself than to her, "The only fear that's to be had when you love someone is the fear of losing them."

I don't even know she's heard me until she answers, her voice strong enough to force me to look back at her, "You're wrong. There are so many different kinds of love."

"I only know one." I stare back at her, my gaze lingering on every inch of her skin until I make my way to the pain in her eyes. This is my fault. It's time that I pay for it.

"I wish I weren't afraid of you," she confesses, her voice distorted by raw pain.

"That makes two of us, little mouse." It takes a deep inhale before I can get the rest out. "I'm sorry I brought you into this." My voice shakes as I say words that sound like goodbye. My sweet Delilah rages against the cuffs for the first time, the metal clanking against the iron frame as she attempts to pull herself upright, but it's no use. She's not getting out of there, not until Walsh comes to get her.

"I never should have come near you." I utter the confession

as Delilah shakes her head, her wild eyes refuting it.

"No," she exclaims. "Stop talking, stop it!"

"I'll leave you alone. I won't hurt you again." I speak aloud what I know to be right, even as my vision blurs and my chest seems to hollow with agony.

"Marcus, I'll call you Marcus!" she screams over top of my apology. "Please don't leave me!" she cries out, fresh tears spilling. "Please, Marcus, please," she begs me, her body arching in protest.

I am a weak man as my grip tightens on the doorframe, so close to leaving her like I know I should. "Please, Marcus, please! Don't leave me!

"Walsh will come for you."

"Please! I want you! Please!"

She wants me. I let the soothing balm of her words calm a piece inside of me that longs for her affection. I know it's only because of the predicament she's in. Cuffed to a bed in a broken-down house, all alone and in the dark, she'd seek comfort from anyone. But still I hesitate to leave.

"Don't leave me," she whimpers, her head hanging low and her words weakened by defeat.

"I told you, little mouse," I say and look back to see her, really see her and what I've done to her. "We all break."

She screams out as I close the door behind me, striding as far away from her as I can to dim her cries. It won't take her long to quiet, I'm sure.

I don't give myself time to think; I text Walsh my address without allowing another moment to pass for me to reconsider, to hold onto hope that I'm wrong.

I watch the clock, knowing he's nearly an hour away.

Curiosity gets the better of me when her cries turn silent. I have to know she's all right more than anything else. She couldn't possibly hurt herself, but still, I have to be sure.

Although her shoulders rise and fall with deep, unsteady breaths, her eyes stay closed as the door creeps open.

The comforter's slipped down her body and I use that as an excuse to bring it up around her shoulders. She's still as I do, but I know she's awake when she slightly leans into my touch. She keeps her lips pressed tight as her bottom lip trembles. The plea is so close to being spoken.

Slowly, I lie down behind her. And when I do, an inhale of relief greets me, her lips parting and her body slightly gravitating toward mine, her back to my front.

It reminds me of the night I first lay with her, when I told her to close her eyes.

If only we had the luxury of living our entire lives like that, in blissful ignorance.

It's selfish to lie down with her. Everything about her calms me. With my eyes closed, I breathe her in, knowing it'll be the last time. I wish that the memory of this moment would comfort me, but given how I have to be careful of her bruises and that I'm the one who made her cry last, this moment will only serve as a reminder to why I should stay far away.

We breathe in unison and it's her steady breaths that calm mine. When I kiss the curve of her neck, she whispers that she loves me, and I believe her, I really do.

So much so, that it lulls me to sleep beside her.

It's not until the door creaks open and my brother stares back at me, that I wake up, my eyes tired and full of shame.

"I didn't mean to be here," I confess to him as his eyes widen with unspoken questions. I do my best not to wake her as I creep out of bed and turn away from him. His weight shifts at the door, causing the floorboards to creak.

"Just get her to her sister."

Cody nods in agreement and I walk past him, neither of us saying another word as I leave him to save her from this nightmare in a way I never can escape.

Chapter 15

Delilah

"I'm begging you." My sister's voice is strained as I sit in her office. The faint bruise on my left arm is barely there anymore. I've traced it idly this past week. It's the last remaining reminder of what happened. Physically speaking, that is.

"Cody begged you, and now I'm begging." The mention of Cody's name does something to me. There's a place inside my chest that's felt empty for days. I can barely look at him. I know he wants me still, and he blames himself when he shouldn't. I told him he shouldn't. My sister told him to give me time. But time isn't going to change any of this.

Her voice is thick with embitterment when she says, "For Christ's sake, do you want me to get down on my knees?"

"Is this because I asked to meet you here instead of your

apartment?" I know damn well she's not pushing the issue just because I don't want to go back to her apartment. Still, it's a defense. The reason she wants me to go into therapy is multifaceted but she understands I didn't want to go back to her place, and have this conversation in the place I was abducted.

I'll be fine if I never go back there again.

My sister starts in again. "You didn't go to mom's funeral. You aren't sleeping."

"And how would you know that?" I question snidely, even though she's right.

"You look like hell, Delilah." I scoff at her comment. "And you should," she stresses, almost as if an apology.

"You went through hell, so it makes sense that you'd look like it."

"Well, thanks for that," I say and pull my purse into my lap, sitting stiffly on a very comfortable sofa draped in deep blue velvet. The clock above my sister's desk ticks away as she sighs, both frustrated and saddened. "You need to talk to someone. It doesn't have to be me."

Playing with the thin necklace that drapes across my décolleté, I do my best to consider what she's asking me to do. She wants me to tell all my secrets to someone like her. A man or a woman who supposedly won't judge me, yet they'll have the option to give me pills if they deem them fit.

Isn't that a part of judgment? Sighing to myself, I ask her, "Do you really think it's going to help me?"

I know what would help me, but he's not answering me. I have no way to see him, no way to make any of this better.

"I'm seeing someone," my sister says and leans forward, "after mom ..." She leaves the word *dying* unspoken, leaning back in her seat. The leather groans as she continues, "And what happened with our father."

I can't bear the mention of our father. Staring past my sister's cream blouse, I focus on the textured wallpaper that lines her office. It's a simple damask pattern in a pale blue and cream colorway.

"Don't bring up Dad, please." Cadence's shoulders sag slightly, her brow raising in condolence. I didn't realize how much she loathed him until I saw her reaction to the news that our father was a serial killer.

Beyond a moment of surprise, she believed every word to be true without hesitation.

I still don't know what I believe.

He took the fall for all those murders. Some of those murders, though, really were his handiwork. Without a doubt, I know he must've killed them. I remember the names of some of those women. They news was peppered with them when I was younger. A series of young girls going missing, each time happening closer to home, and a public outcry for their bodies to be found.

I remember the way my mother stared at the television, demanding my sister and I never stay out late and always check in even though we were so much younger than the victims. There's no way she knew my father committed those murders. At least not then, but somehow, I think she found out. Or maybe she only suspected.

I wish she were alive so I could ask her. I wish I knew what she was thinking and why she stayed with him if she thought he'd killed them.

"You know he did it, don't you?" My sister's question brings me back to the here and now, and the faint memories of childhood vanish. "Did you read the articles?"

"I read them," I lie.

"The parts about you aren't true."

"I know," I say to go along with her although I imagine some parts are true; not in black and white, but they're true in the gray areas. Maybe because I know the truth and I'm holding it in. Therefore, whatever comes out is most certainly a lie.

"There's no evidence that you were involved. They can't pin a thing on you. It's all—"

"Circumstantial," I say, finishing the sentence for her. "I know," I repeat, my voice quieter and the fight in her eyes draining.

"It's not okay that anyone thinks you were a part of any of this."

The steady ticking of the clock passes between us before my sister starts up again, saying, "You're not okay."

"I know."

"What if ..." she starts with a hint of optimism and leaves her place in the wingback chair across from me to round her desk. The drawer opens and closes quickly enough, and she presents me with a pale blue journal.

"What if you put whatever you're feeling in this?"

"You therapists and your journals." It has the softest leather cover, but it feels like betrayal in my palms.

"I'll feel better if you'll tell me you'll at least try," she says, attempting a compromise. Her tone is telling, as if she's certain this is the solution. "If things get bad or start to slip even the slightest ... will you come talk to me?"

"So you can be my shrink?" My response is both dismissive and playful. "I thought you got a promotion and you won't have time for patients?"

Her smile makes me smile. It's humble and small, but I know this is a big deal for Cadence. "The Rockford Center won't be open for another month. So I can't start my position there just yet, but it'll be nice to be in a brand-new facility and with patients who ..."

She trails off and the smile fades. My sister is a hero in so many ways. In ways I could never be. Christopher's face flashes before my eyes and I nearly lose it on the spot. It takes everything in me to hide the swell of emotions.

"Well, you know." She sucks in a breath and relaxes her posture then asks, "What's going on with you and Cody?

Have you talked to him at least?"

I struggle to answer her honestly, so I deflect, although I'm sure she's well aware that's what I'm doing. "I don't have time to think about my sex life right now, not with the board meeting coming up." Another lie. So many damn lies.

The truth about Cody is that it all makes me feel like I've lost my mind.

Love and hate are both insane.

If they were products of a sane mind, the two emotions would be logical and controllable. God knows they aren't.

Chapter 16

Marcus

I've written so many notes with deep strokes that left the paper embossed with names. Too many to know for certain, but at least thousands of letters and hundreds of names. This one is so very different from all the others.

At the top of the page, the blue ink barely touched the notepad. Featherlight script trails down the page, each letter carefully placed. It's not a warning or a message, but a question that I'm not sure she'll answer.

Maybe I'm selfish, but I had to ask her, even if I don't know how she'll respond to it.

Even worse, I'm not sure how to sign it. I don't know which name should appear at the bottom. Which man she'd be willing to meet one last time at the barn where all this began.

Christopher or Marcus. The pen hangs in the air just like the question, and it feels as if my life hovers with them.

It started at the old barn that served as my refuge and then became the hell that raised me ... and it should end there. I'm willing to close this chapter, I'm willing to never write another name down for as long as I live, so long as she'll listen to me. So long as she believes me. I've never wanted anyone to see me and to know my story, the way I crave for her to know every detail. Swallowing thickly, I sign the note and drag air into my lungs. Listening to the crackle of wood splintering and smoldering in the fireplace, I turn to watch the embers burn bright.

This place holds secrets in every corner, moments where I devised plans and sought evidence of justice in the keepsakes I've taken. Although I've parted with a number of them now, all in efforts to put blame elsewhere.

Whether or not Delilah meets me, I'll leave this place and never return. Walsh will wander here, I know he will. He's come many a time in search of me. He's the only one I've met here. He must know it means something to me. After all, I brought the love of our lives here, I mended her here and lay beside her without worry. He will come back. He'll find the note I left for him. Riggins is expecting his call if ever my brother needs anything. I'll leave it all to him.

The knowledge that this address was once the home of a family I sought justice for has escaped him for years.

I had to buy it and live here just so I could sleep after I slaughtered the men who took their daughter and ripped their family apart. After ending their lives, I stole every penny they had and took on their wealth and names for years. Even the deed to this place bears the name of a man who's long dead but according to records, resides elsewhere and the place is thought to be empty, waiting for him when he returns.

I imagine one day I'll forget this address, but I'll always remember her name. For so long, it's the names of the victims that I used to justify what I'd done. I murdered, I stole, I manipulated situations to wreak havoc and send bad men to war against one another. And all of it was justified if I could name their victims.

It's her name, Delilah Jones, that prompts me leaving this place forever.

I simply can't go back. Not after what's happened.

The only other thing I regret is bringing my brother into this. He could have had a different life; instead I led him into the nightmare with me. Delilah and Cody will forever be the names that counter the one I took, Marcus.

I can't do this any longer, but I don't know how my brother will recover. I don't know where any of us will go from here. Which is why I have to meet her one more time.

Crossing out the name at the bottom of the note, I write another there instead.

Maybe she'll realize I'm trying. If that doesn't prove to her that I am willing to do anything to keep her close, I don't know what will.

Chapter 17

Delilah

All I can think as his silhouette comes into view, is whether I'll have the strength to call him Christopher and what he'll do if that name slips from my lips.

He isn't the man in a dark alley they call the grim reaper. He isn't a supervillain with inhuman strength. He's not a demon or the devil. He's a man who was hurt, cut deep and never able to heal. So he bled all over the world, letting all those who he felt wronged him drown in it.

Christopher is a broken man and that scares me, because I don't know how he'll ever heal, but my inner voice screams to help him. Because I irrevocably love him.

"I haven't been able to sleep," I say, ignoring the heavy thoughts when I've made my way to the large oak tree just beyond the barn. The field is barren and recently harvested. In the distance, a sliver of silver stains the background, snow that's yet to melt from the storm this past week. It's cold and lonely and in the dead of winter, there's not a soul out here on the edge of this Podunk town.

The bitter bite in the air has turned the tip of Christopher's charming nose and his high cheekbones a shade of pale pink. Even his chiseled jaw holds a hue of rose. With a black wool coat and dark blue jeans, a hint of stubble on his face and freshly cut hair, he could pretend to be a CEO or businessman and I'd fall for it. Those baby blue eyes of his could fool the best of the world into believing whatever he said.

"You look beautiful, though," he murmurs and eats up the small distance between us with quick strides. I swear I feel warmer just looking at him, even if he is feet away. "Even if you are tired," he adds and then swallows thickly. The nervous energy pricking between us is almost palpable.

I nearly call him by name, telling him I can't do this. Instead I rip my gaze from his, ignoring the stampeding in my chest to search along the tree line for anyone who could be watching. In this position out in the open, we're exposed. Anyone and everyone could see us, if only they knew where to look or bothered to be here. But we're all alone and why would anyone bother to look for us?

I'm of no consequence and my father will forever carry the moniker of serial killer for crimes I know Christopher has committed.

With that thought in my mind, I focus on the building behind Christopher. The run-down barn my father bought years ago is decrepit and in disarray. He didn't keep up with it in the decades since I've left home, that much is obvious.

I tell myself the only reason I came is to forgive Christopher for pinning all those murders on my father. To acknowledge that he saved me and to thank him ... To kiss him one more time. To end a business deal of sorts that we made in a cheap hotel room weeks ago when he told me I would beg for him. He wasn't wrong, but there's no need for such a deal to exist anymore.

The very thought makes my heart ache with longing. Maybe I should confess to him that I don't know what I'll become, but a part of me longs to be with him. That a small voice whispers wherever he would take me, I'd feel at home. Whatever I'd be beside him, I'd feel is right.

He clears his throat and my attention is brought back to him. To his handsome face and the obvious tension between us. It blisters as if we're surrounded by fire, when in reality it's the chill of winter that batters us.

"I don't know how to start," he admits and takes a heavy inhale.

Shoving my hands into my pockets, I clear my throat too and stare down at my feet. I've worn my best pair of heels even though I knew we were meeting at the old farm by my family house. I'd be lying to myself if I said the dress beneath my double-breasted trench coat wasn't picked out just for him, along with the lacy lingerie.

I even chose the dark red shade because I know the color complements and suits my caramel skin. I wear it on every first date, and yet I chose to wear it this evening. As the sun sets, leaving us little light, and the cold surrounds us, daring me to expose the deep-V of my bra. As if I would.

Embarrassment rises inside of me. "Whatever you have to say," I tell him, "just say it."

There's a pain that flashes across his face, and I have to admit, I feel it deep in the marrow of my bones as well.

It must mean something, I tell myself, when you can't stand to say that final goodbye. He takes another step forward, and before I can deny him or even think twice, he leans forward, closing his eyes and I close mine too, my entire being relaxing from the gentle kiss. My coat rustles as I reach out to him, letting the cold hit my hands as I splay them against his chest, wishing we were anywhere else.

The kiss surprises me, as does my reaction to it. These last few nights I've dreamed of him, but it's only this side I can accept. The other things ... what he's done and why he's done them, they still scare me. They terrify me. The version of him now, lures me to sleep. The other half of him is what wakes me in the middle of the night with violent screams chasing my breath.

"This is for you." Christopher's words are whispered, his lips pressing against mine just slightly until he pulls back, making me lean forward and subconsciously I rise onto my tiptoes, needing more and unable to break the kiss.

He does end it, though, leaving me longing and my heart pounding in my chest. A fear slips into my blood, raging as my pulse quickens. There's something here between us, some sense of pain that threatens to drown me if ever I didn't have this man.

Before I can bear to speak the thought in my mind, that this moment isn't a goodbye, that the kiss he just placed on my lips wasn't the last we'll share, Christopher pulls out a small box.

It's simple by design and plastic. He doesn't hesitate to pull back the lid and apart from a silver hinge, the only thing in the box is a small red button.

"What is it?"

"It breaks me every time I come here and I didn't know why … I didn't know why I couldn't stand to be here and how I questioned everything when I thought about this barn."

"This barn?" A deep crease settles between my brow as my mind races for an explanation as if I should already know what Christopher means.

"I learned from your father. I came here, lived here and I watched everything he did." The confession wreaks havoc on my consciousness, on the memories I have of my father. No.

I'm quick to deny it all. He's lying.

"Christopher," I say and his name is a warning, one that pulls me from the shock of his confession. "I know my father ... he ... I don't know what he did but ..." My head shakes on its own, the small child inside of me screaming that whatever the man in front of me is about to say, it's not true.

It doesn't take more than a second to pass, before I know that it is true, though. He wouldn't lie to me. Christopher wouldn't fill my head with a tale that could destroy me. Not if he could help it.

He's silent and it's then I notice the small box trembles in his hand. Tears gloss over and the vision of him, the man in the shadows, the man who's done so much wrong in this world, it blurs.

"I want to share it with you," he whispers. Swiping quickly under my eyes, I pull myself together, standing straighter and steadying my breath. "I have to. I have to tell someone." His swallow is audible and there's a vulnerability in his eyes, one that shines in his sharp blue eyes, begging not to be denied.

"I'm here," I answer him in a ragged whisper, still coping with my own truth and realizations, straightening my shoulders and praying that if nothing else, a confession will heal a small piece of him. I'm desperate for that mending to take place. More than my own sanity, I crave for him to be well.

"It's going to take more than one conversation, I'm afraid," he tells me, leaving the question hanging there and before I can ask it, he gives it life. "I need time and I want it with you. I need to," he pauses and stares past me, and then glances over his shoulder at the barn. "I need to acknowledge what happened."

"What happened?" I dare to ask him and instead of answering, he brings the plastic box up higher and asks me, "Will you destroy it? Would you destroy the barn because I wanted it to end?"

My eyes widen with the question and I take a half step back. "It's a bomb?" I breathe out at the realization, letting him hear my fear.

"It's an ending," he offers me, his voice strained. "Would you let it end if it meant that tomorrow I would seek you out? Every day after, I would go where you went and tell you every secret and every confession. I would give you everything if you would let me. But would you end this piece so I never had to see it again? So I could let it rest?"

There's nothing but agony in his question, a strength that's undeniable, but it's crippled by pain. "Please," he adds, "would you do it for me?"

The need to put an end to his pain is greater than any fear. I didn't recognize it as a truth until my hand reached out, my fingers covering the back of his hand and my thumb pressing on the button without a word spoken. There's a soft click as the button is pressed, my inhale nearly a gasp. As he steps forward, a hand wrapping around my back, I wish I could watch as the sight unfolded.

The bang of an explosion that rips a shocked, sharp breath from me. The base of the building giving out and the clatter of what nearly sounds like thunder surrounding us. It's a violent moment, destruction claiming the building and the warmth of fire felt far too soon as it engulfs the building.

But as it is, I can't pull my eyes away from his hungry gaze. As the building collapses and flames rage in the distance, only a few hundred feet away, I'm held captive by Christopher and the intense pull and spark between us.

He's the one to break it. To let the box fall to the ground as the burning rubble collapses in the distance. He's the one to grip my hips and pull me closer so he can crash his lips against mine. His touch is possessive and just as hot and smoldering as the fire.

I'm the one to take it further, though, slipping my hands through his coat and up his shirt, desperate for my skin to be against his. He follows suit, pulling my coat open and dropping his lips lower, trailing down my throat and along my collarbone.

"I need you," he groans against my skin and I've never been so thankful to hear those words.

It's a storm of chaos as he drops me to the ground. The desire is at odds with every move he makes. Hovering over me, caging me in, yet savoring our deepened kiss with the low groans of a satisfied man. Carefully lifting my coat, he only uncovers what he needs to gain access, slowly slipping my underwear down and all the while his gaze stays on mine, waiting for my reaction.

"Please," I beg him in a whisper, such a soft sound compared to the chaos just beyond us, but it feels as if I screamed the plea. It's the only sound that matters. Lowering his lips to the crook of my neck, he runs my arousal over my clit in steady circles before moving his fingers lower and teasing me.

Pleasure ripples through my body, forcing me to arch my back. The heat wars against the bitter cold in the air. As I moan my pleasure, Christopher silences me with a kiss. This one is different from all the others—gentle, caressing yet possessive. As he pulls away, I stare into his piercing gaze and then my lips part in a silent scream. He enters me in a swift stroke, completely and fully, his own lips parting and a deep rumble of lust leaving his throat.

It's painful, thrilling and gratifying all at once. The heat takes over every inch of me as he moves. His thrusts are forceful, but each time he kisses me, peppering them on my skin with a delicacy that doesn't match his motions, I need more. It's sweet, agonizing torture as he pushes the impending threat of my orgasm higher and higher.

We're both out of breath when he finds his release, my nails scratching down his back as I cry out his name.

Smoke billows steadily from the rubble of the barn, and

the scent is carried along gusts of wind. The chill returns faster than I thought it would, but then again I've never been a few hundred yards from a raging fire of destruction.

"You meant it didn't you, when you said you'd come find me? That you'd stay with me?" I know he didn't say those exact words; *stay* was never spoken from his lips, but that's what I want from him. I don't want him to leave because I'm afraid he won't come back. Selfishly, I would sleep better if I knew he was beside me. I would sleep so deeply feeling him lay next to me.

"I think you need time to decide what you want."

"And if I want you to stay?"

"If you want me to stay, I'll stay."

"I want to leave this place. I want—"

"Give it time. You need to know so much more than you do. The only thing I ask is that you don't tell anyone who I am."

I almost tell him I'd never tell anyone he was Marcus, but he continues and what he says feels like a knife to the heart.

"I'm not ready to be Christopher. If you have to tell my name to someone, I'd rather be anyone else ... I'd rather be Cody. Please," he whispers, "don't tell them what really happened. I'd rather be Cody and if you could lie for me, I'll tell you everything, give you everything and be whoever you need me to be. I'm just not ready to be Christopher again."

My tears slip down my cheeks silently as I watch him staring at the flames subsiding in the distance. "Please promise me, Delilah. You can call me Christopher, but don't tell anyone. Please. I'd rather be anyone else to all of them."

I try to hide the pain in my voice as I whisper, "I promise" and wipe away the tears, as if they were never there.

Chapter 18

Delilah

How many times this week will I utter the words "I love you," and yet it feels like I'm saying goodbye?

"Please tell me what happens," my sister urges me and my throat feels tight as I stand outside the mahogany wood doors with the phone pressed to my ear. The foreboding doors extend from floor to ceiling in the hall.

It's not these exact doors that I laid eyes on when I first experienced the awe of what was just behind them. The courtroom and the men who brought justice to those who desperately needed it. But they're all the same, aren't they? All these doors.

When I was a child, they intimidated me, as did the men who sat beside my father on the other side of them. Now, though, they're only doors I don't wish to ever step through again. They hold no meaning any longer.

"Did you hear me, Delilah?" My sister's voice brings me back to the present.

"Hmm?"

"Tell me what happens."

My answer is far too even, far too calm for the lie it is when I say, "Of course I will."

I could already tell her the outcome, though. I won't fight it. The accusations aren't true, but I won't fight them. With what little I have left, there's not an ounce of me that gives a damn to fight the charges brought against me.

Ending the call with an honest *I love you*, I pocket my phone and face the board that will address the charges and my standing in this courtroom.

Their voices drone on with their stern expression reflecting revulsion or concern as my gaze travels down each of the faces I recognize so well. Men and women I strived to earn a position beside.

It feels like that was a lifetime ago.

"Miss Jones, you realize that we are discussing disbarment?"

"I do."

"Do you have anything at all that you'd like to say?"

"It was an honor," I say and my tone is respectable, but there's not a bit of fight in it. All that I was is no longer recognizable in the echoing chamber of this room. "It was an honor to prosecute alongside you all."

"Do you not deny the unethical nature of your recent actions and the speculation of criminal activity?" The question comes out incredulously.

"You didn't do this." My friend, boss, and mentor's eyes are wide as she makes the statement. Her expression is one of complete shock.

"I urge you to reconsider—" Another member of the board who appears more confused than anything attempts to bring order to the room as murmurs erupt.

"It is her mental health," Claire pipes up again. She isn't wrong, but I'm not willing to go back to the reality I once held so close to my heart.

Malden rebuts Claire's assertion, saying, "There is no evidence to support that and you do not speak on her behalf."

"Delilah, say something," Claire's command is more of a plea. Her ever-imposing features are distraught. "You did not do what you are being accused of," she speaks clearly and her tone is far more stable than it was a moment ago, but the crease in her brow and sorrow in her eyes tell me she's anything other than balanced. She's on edge. They all are.

The five of them stare back at me from where they sit and I feel nothing. I represented them and this court. I failed them. If nothing else, I can admit to that.

The tension in the room is all for them. I feel nothing.

"I am content with the board's decision that I am not fit to practice law." I practiced that statement this morning. I practiced speaking it calmly and clearly. It is my decision and it is best that I never hold any power of convincing others what is right and what is wrong again. "I am not fit for it."

"For the moment—" Claire emphasizes with a pleading tone as she stands to her feet. The words aren't meant for me. Her palms are on the large conference table as she leans over. "She cannot be held to the standards of the court when her mental state is in question."

"Without any evidence from Miss Jones to support your statement that she isn't mentally well, or any—"

"We have not even done an investigation!" Claire's voice rises and all four men stare down the table at her. She's losing it, her emotions getting the best of her. I wish she wouldn't fight for me.

There's a moment of deadened silence. It seems to dawn on her that it's four against one. There's a part of me that feels guilty, but if she knew the truth, she wouldn't take my side in this. She'd join those four men and take their judgment in stride.

"The charges brought against her are severe and there does not appear to be any defense other than your claims that she is not well, Miss Eastings." The argument progresses. Four against one until Claire heaves in a steadying breath and adjusts her blouse before taking her seat once again. She's worn the look of defeat many times, but never did it age her like it does now.

I wish I could tell her I was sorry. If I could lie in this moment, I'd thank her and apologize for not fighting by her side as she speaks up for me. The reverence and compassion are still met with gratitude just the same, but I cannot lie. I'm not sorry to allow this to happen. I'm not sorry to be silent now and accept their judgment. I never want to cross beyond doors like ones behind me after I leave today. Never again.

Her passion should be saved for someone else. Someone who needs a voice to fight for them. Someone who's gone through hell and once they've reached the end of it, they remain surrounded by a fire that holds them hostage until someone stronger can put it out.

Those people exist. The devil staying by their side to torment them with the memories of what injustice has been done to them. They surround us every day, hiding their pain and carrying on as if they're like us, but they aren't. The pain consumes them and they're the ones she should save her passion for. Not me.

I knew what I was doing, and I walked into that purgatory after a flame that singed my mind. The devil still walks beside me, but I choose him for comfort.

"The complicit nature of your actions regarding your father's death and potential crimes surrounding it and many others that have been recently opened with new information previously held in, not only your father's possession, but openly in your family home ..."

There are over fifty cases that he refers to. Fifty names that are now etched in stone lying in quiet graveyards.

This bar cannot be tainted with someone who worked so closely with so much injustice.

"This information that's been brought to our attention and the formal complaint brought against you ... it's," he says, then with an audible exhale, Malden finishes, "it's alarming to say the least."

"What you do today could affect your ability to defend yourself in these cases, Delilah," Claire pleads with me once more, her eyes glossy and the corners of her thinning lips turned down.

"I didn't—" I nearly defend myself, I nearly explain to her simply because she's more than a boss and a friend, she's someone who will need answers. It's who she is; I should know because it's who I used to be.

My shoulders rise as my lungs fill with a steadying breath. "I make no statement. I will not participate in the investigation and I have no desire to refute any complaints that have been brought forward."

"Miss Jones, you have to know," David Perry speaks. He's another lawyer, older, the same age my father would be.

"I accept whatever decision the board makes."

"She is not well," Claire says once again, although she

doesn't rise from her seat and her fingers lace together in front of her.

All I can think, as the discussion continues without my voice being needed, is that I loved this. I loved all of this for so long. It's yet another love that has turned to goodbye.

With their voices muted and my vision blurring, the crack of wood split with the hiss of a fire envelops me. The flames rage in the back of my mind, wild and untamed. A piece of my sanity whispers, it's unethical as well. My passion is buried with the soot of what happened in the last months. My fervor is no longer logical, it is not black and white and line by line of precedence and rules. The burning need for justice is still there, not even buried beneath the surface, I feel it still and I doubt that will ever change.

Regardless of what these men and woman say today or tomorrow, I am not fit any longer, but not for any reason they could possibly imagine.

Maybe if they knew our story, all of it from every one of us, they'd realize I should have never been in a courtroom. I wasn't meant for a life of what is right and wrong. My life was meant for one moment, one travesty that created a ripple of transgressions.

Chapter 19

Cody

It's not the worst thing in the world, I think to myself.

As if resigning is what's on my mind. As if that's what has me staring forward at a battered dartboard across the bar. The lively room is at odds with every emotion that's dim and muted inside of me. This constant loss that seems to only hollow out more and more of me as the days wear on.

I have nothing left. That's all I can think. Every piece of my world crumbled so quickly and without any chance at all of me stopping the wreckage. It was foolish for me to think I had any control at all or that I could keep up with the lies and sins.

With every tick of the clock, I accept my role and how I set the pieces into motion. I let each cog of the wheel turn, only watching as the time passed and the inevitable occurred.

There's a rousing cheer from my left, a group of men happily clinking their bottles together in celebration of whatever just played on the televisions that line that wall.

At one point, I would pretend to share their sentiment, for no other reason than to blend in so I could continue to hide my secrets in plain sight.

Now, though, I seem to prefer fading. It feels ... justified to say the least.

Ghosts of a glass filled with white wine and an easy laugh sit at the end of the bar where I first laid eyes on Delilah. I knew then the person I was and still, I tainted her. I remember how she twirled a curl of her hair between her fingers that night years ago. I remember how she glanced at me. I remember thinking I could never give in. And yet ... I did. Now all I have left are memories that never should have been.

Even as another patron takes the seat next to mine, a beer in both hands, one for him and one for the woman beside him, all I think about is her.

The scent of white wine and florals that drifted from her when we sat across from one another at a high-top table like this. The night she first kissed me will haunt me forever.

For what it did to her and the series of events that followed, I can't bring myself to feel anything but a deluge of regret.

"There you are." Delilah's voice is amiable, which doesn't fit right on her. Even the grace of a gentle smile in greeting only adds to the loneliness.

With her small hand raised, the bartender recognizes her and brings over a glass. All the while we wait in silence and I drink her in.

"How are you?" I ask the simple question and I never realized how much it means to me. To go days without knowing and suffering in each moment that I question it, it truly carries the weight of the world in three small words that are so commonly spoken without regard.

"I'm not okay," she admits, a sadness seemingly lifting up the corners of her lips before she takes a sip of the sweet wine. Her dark red lipstick leaves an imprint on the clear glass.

"Is there anything I can do?" I ask, wishing I could go back and fix it all. But just like shards of a broken mirror, it'll never be the same again even if I could mend all the pieces and make it seemingly whole once more.

She only shakes her head slightly and then her amber eyes meet mine. "How are you?"

"I've been better," I answer although I hold so much back. How is it that even after all of this, I still can't give her the honesty that begs to be spoken?

"I'm sorry," she whispers and retreats to her wine, admitting, "I wish I knew how to make it better, but I don't."

"You're with him?" I have to ask. I have to know for sure. Seeing him in bed with her ... I can't wrap my mind around it. How I could love someone so deeply, yet hold back because someone else needs her love more. It's as if I'm wrapped in barbed wire and I don't know how it happened or how to escape, but either way, I simply stay as still as I can so the razors don't cut any deeper.

"I was," she answers and both of us watch her thin fingers glide down the stem of the glass. "I was with him yesterday," she tells me.

"You love him?"

With her hair pulled away from her face, styled in a high bun and her sheer black blouse hanging delicately off her shoulders, she can't hide her expression. It's one that clearly displays sorrow. Not for herself; the melancholy is saved for me.

"I do," she answers simply and then takes in an uneasy breath, pushing her half glass of wine away from her. "I didn't mean for any of this—"

"I know," I say, cutting her off and turning my body to face the bar so I can stare straight ahead at the worn wooden dartboard once again. "I didn't mean for it to happen either."

Even as I feel her slipping away, I haven't a clue what to say to her. Everything that comes to mind would only make things worse, it would only tangle the wire that much tighter around my throat. I have to say something, though.

"You know, even if I'm not with you, even if you never kiss me again, I'll still love you." The feeling of loss coats my confession. "You know that, don't you?"

"Funny." She manages a sad smile that doesn't reach her eyes. "I was about to say the same to you, but it sounded too much like goodbye."

"I never did like goodbyes," I comment if for no other reason than to end it, but she doesn't let it go.

"You'll let me go? You'll be all right if I'm with him? You won't hate me?"

"I promise. I'll be all right. I'll let you go." With a nod, she accepts my answer and the air is different between us.

"Another drink?" I ask even though hers isn't gone yet.

She only nods, her eyes turning glossy. "Another drink."

CHAPTER 20

DELILAH

A hot shower can wash away a world of hurt. Something about the cleansing heat lies to the mind and whispers that it's all gone, it's all going to be all right and that the filth and dirt that wish to linger won't come back tomorrow.

Even with my eyes wide open staring at the tile in my shower, I listen to the promises and let myself believe it's all behind us now.

Taking my time, I dry myself without a hurry to do a damn thing. I let my lush curls create a halo around my face and accept myself for all that I've become.

When I step out of the bathroom and the red dials of the clock blink in the telling fashion that the power's been tripped, I feel the pull of a soft smile.

I don't think of my gun; there isn't an ounce of fear that runs through me. Instead there's a warmth of knowing. Maybe it's because I feel his presence already. The air is different—easier, calmer and more peaceful. As if he alone is my fate and what makes it all make sense.

There is no thinking, no torture, no pain. Only him and I.

"Have you thought about it?" he asks me and I hum an answer as I open the top drawer in search of something to wear. With the towel still wrapped around me, I settle on a simple black satin camisole and matching boy shorts.

"Have I thought about what?" I question back without even seeing Christopher yet. The towel drops around my feet in a heap with a soft thud and when I look up Christopher's waiting for me, stalking toward me.

He takes his time to place a palm on the dresser on either side of me, essentially caging me in. "You know what," he answers and places a small kiss on my bare shoulder before pushing off and taking his place on the end of the bed.

One thing I've noticed in the past few days is how he doesn't stay still for long until I lie down with him. Then it's as if we could remain together forever.

"I was thinking of something," he says, letting the previous conversation go for a moment. As I slip on the cami, I keep my eyes on him.

"What's that?"

Falling back onto the bed, he watches the fan spin above

it as he tells me, "I remembered this plate. You know the switch plates for light switches in children's rooms?"

"The wall plate?"

"Yeah," he answers and I still don't know where he's going with this.

"Yeah, I know them."

"I don't remember much about my parents, or my aunt really. But I remembered last night that I had a wall plate of this cartoon character in my bedroom when I was a kid, and I think it was at my aunt's house too."

"A wall plate ... what made you think of that?"

"I was just wondering what my parents would think. And I remember they loved me. They loved me so much they screwed a cheap switch plate on the wall with some cartoon dog on it. I barely remember living with my aunt, but I think she took the switch plate and put it up too."

I'm careful with my words. I've never talked to Christopher about his family. With Cody I only ever spoke about his uncle and even those conversations were short. He's not well and the last Cody spoke of him, he'd forgotten who Cody was. "You've been thinking about your childhood?"

"I was wondering why ... you know ... why it happened and if there was any sign that I would be like this before I was taken."

"And?" I prod him for more after a long moment of quiet.

"And all I remember is how much I loved that stupid wall

plate and that my mother was the last one to kiss me good night and turn off the light. I remember watching her do it."

"I don't think I had a wall plate that I remember, but I had wallpaper of pink polka dots, just a few inches off from the ceiling."

"Sounds like a nightmare," he comments and I let out a small huff of a laugh.

"Do you want to keep talking about it?" I ask him, reaching for my face cream, but hesitating to open it. I made a deal with myself. If he talks, I'll take it. If he doesn't, then I'll talk. I'll learn his secrets, and he'll learn mine.

"I want to know if you'll come with me? For a short while?"

"Where are you going?"

"Somewhere away from here. Away from what I'm used to. Some place that doesn't have memories hiding in every corner. Would that be all right? I ... I can't stay here any longer. Not when everything looks so different but I can't be anything other than what I've been."

I'm not sure how my sister will feel if I leave again. Biting the inside of my cheek, I don't comment on that or acknowledge my thoughts of his brother.

Instead I reach for a small plastic bag on my dresser. "I bought something today," I tell him and that gets his attention.

"You want to open it or should I just show you?" I ask him and he stands slowly, taking his time as his eyes narrow suspiciously.

"Show me," he commands and makes his way back to me. The bit of curiosity that adds to his charm vanishes when I pull the cuffs from the bag. They're simple metal, just like the ones he has.

The tension thickens, and his swallow is audible. "For you or for me?" It's a serious question and I knew his reaction might not be one of an eager man.

"For me. For you to cuff me to the bed and for me to—"

"I don't need that, Delilah."

"I do, though," I stress. "I can admit it and I need you to know that." Any indication that he'll refuse leaves us. "I need this and I need you to do it." I've dreamed about being cuffed underneath him, I've felt that fear and then a mix of desire. "I mean it. I want this."

"You want me to cuff you to the bed?" he questions with his chest pressed against my shoulders. He destroys the distance between us until my bare back all the way down to the swell of my ass is pressed against him. "And then what?" he asks, fully giving in to my wish.

"Whatever you want," I whisper, meeting his sharp heated gaze in the mirror of my dresser. His head falls forward, his lips brushing against the shell of my ear. As he plants a soft kiss there, I add, "You can do what you want to me."

He groans in the crook of my neck and the vibrations travel from his warm breath there all the way down to the most forbidden places.

"I accept your gift of cuffs then," he says, lifting his gaze to meet mine in the mirror and we share a devilish simper between us. I can get lost in him and he can get lost in me. Together we'll heal each other. That's the only hope I'm holding on to. Everything else can fade away and burn for all I care.

Well, almost everything else. We still have our family.

"Have you thought about my question?"

"If I'm willing to go with you?"

"If you don't come with me, I don't know that I can leave. I don't know what will happen to you. I wouldn't be able to live with myself not knowing."

"How long will we be gone?"

"Not long. We'll keep your place; we'll visit. I never could go long without seeing my brother."

"Do you think he'll stay?" I ask him in all seriousness.

"I don't know, I haven't heard from him."

"You reached out?"

"I did. I apologized." The ever-present knife in my chest twists at the knowledge that Cody didn't respond to Christopher. One day I hope the two of them will be all right. One day they'll work together and be side by side.

"I'm sorry."

He kisses my cheek quickly and then stands up straight behind me, his fingers trailing down my arm ever so gently. "It's not your fault," he tells me but that doesn't mean I can't be sorry.

I know his secrets. I know his pain. Even if I've never felt it like he has on his skin, I feel it in my soul. It's etched in the crevices of my bones.

He doesn't have to whisper them. They're written in his piercing eyes, the shards of light blue reflecting the agony of years of pain.

"I see you for who you are. And I love you. You love me?"

"Of course I do. I've always loved you."

Chapter 21

Delilah

Ten months later

His gaze is sharp; he has the most piercing blue eyes I've ever seen. As I freeze where I'm standing in the middle of the aisle, the faint noise of dull music mixed with the sound of carts rolling by fades into the background. It all blurs together in aisle four of the grocery store as my grip on the loaf of bread I'm holding turns so clammy that the plastic slips.

The pitter-patter of my racing heart and my blood rushing in my ears is all I can hear.

Nothing else matters. I can feel his eyes on me. Every time I blink, I see them, surrounded by shadows.

I take my time, placing the items from my cart back on

the shelves with trembling fingers. There are only four things seeing as how I just got here, a bag of rice being the first item to go back on the bottom shelf before I slowly and meticulously roll my cart to the end of the only aisle I've been down.

It's chilling, the fear that rolls down my spine knowing he's watching me. Feeling him again. *Is it fear, though?* My heart beats wildly in response to the question, fighting and railing against the decision to act calm. I can't let anyone know. I just need to get out of here ... So we can be alone.

My heart isn't afraid, not like my logical side is. When the shadow is just barely seen, tall and foreboding, my stomach drops and my heart flips with recognition. It's an undeniable feeling when you miss someone you know you shouldn't. I try to focus on the sound of wheels squeaking against the linoleum floor and the noisy clang of metal from carts being lined up in order to help ground me.

"Do you need any help?" The question comes from a young man in a red vest that barely hides the nondescript black logo on his white shirt beneath it. I recognize him; I've seen him a number of times in this grocery store. I'm certain he's rung me up a handful of times since I returned here a month ago.

How did I think I could move back, even if the house is on the outskirts in the middle of nowhere, and *he* wouldn't find me? How could I be so foolish to think he wouldn't come for me?

A sinking feeling in my chest moves my hand there, and the paper list in my hand crinkles as I do. I'd forgotten all about it and as I gaze down at the blurred pen lines and wrinkled paper, I do my best to school my expression.

"Oh, no," I say and my throat is too tight as I speak. I close my eyes, forcing a simple smile to my lips and clear my throat. "I just realized something," I answer, finally looking the young man in his deep brown eyes. "I have a call in ten minutes and I'm going to take it in my car then come back," I lie, that smile staying in place although everything in my body wants me to run. Run from here, get far away from other people.

The young man, who looks like he's college age or maybe younger, offers me a friendly smile in return. "Understood," he says with a nod and returns to lining up stacks of carts with the one I've just brought back up front.

Even now, as I take each deliberate step through the glass double doors that slide open automatically as I approach and feel the cool breeze of early spring against my heated face, I try to rid myself of the memories that flash before my eyes.

The bar. The drinks. The feel of a chilled glass of white wine mixed with the scent of whiskey from the man next to me. The court cases and late nights spent getting lost in bed with a man I knew I shouldn't be with. The flirtation, rules being broken.

My heels click as I remember losing my law license, as every dreadful moment returns with the stain of blood. So much blood. Acts of passion that couldn't be taken back. The pain that's already present mingles with so much more.

Wrapping my arms around myself, I attempt to protect my body from the wind but it's useless. The weather isn't what batters me.

The remembrance of his lips on mine and the searing heat of his light touch, force a gasp from me. It's a short one full of longing, knowing those moments are now nothing more than lost ghosts of the person I was. Of the people we were before it all went to hell.

All of the memories are a cocktail that infuses into my conscious thoughts as I listen to my keys clink while I unlock the door to my sedan with a low beep that fills the practically vacant lot. From the time I entered the grocery store to now, a mere fifteen minutes at that, the sun has decided to set, casting a shade of red across the dark tree line of thick forest beyond the store parking lot and stealing the light that was here only a moment ago.

The leather seat groans and the door shuts with a loud thud. All I can do is sit here, my purse now on the console. My keys in my right hand, resting against my lap with the metal digging into my palm since I'm gripping them so tight. My breathing comes in faster and faster although I'm doing everything in my power to stay calm. *He'll be here soon.*

When I hear the click of the back door opening, the one behind my seat, I close my eyes. He didn't make me wait long.

He enters the car accompanied by a chill from the evening wind and the car rocks gently until he's seated behind me and the door is shut. His scent fills my lungs first and as it does, I remember that I've been told that smell is the sense that holds the most memory. Maybe I read it somewhere, but I've never known something to be truer than that fact is now.

When I open my eyes, his chilling gaze is on mine in the rearview mirror and my treacherous heart chokes me in an attempt to escape. It hovers at the base of my throat, pounding viciously in protest.

I did always love him. There wasn't a moment that I didn't love him.

He knows that. He has to know that I still love him; we just simply couldn't be together. We decided. We decided together.

"You said you'd let me go," I whisper, speaking over my strangled breaths.

My gaze never leaves his, even as tears prick my eyes. Not until he answers me.

"I changed my mind."

"You don't get to do that, Cody," I say and my cadence is melancholier than I'd hoped it would come out.

Life is unfair. It's uncertain and torturous. It takes and gives without remorse. I'm grateful for what I have with Christopher, but damn does it hurt to see Cody as he is. Left wanting and alone. He doesn't deserve that, but I can't give him what he deserves. Not when I love someone else the way I do.

If I can't give him my whole heart, he deserves to have someone else's.

I can easily give Christopher everything; it feels as if it's always been his to have. That is life and that is love. I accept it now, the simplicity yet the sheer magnitude of it. Because I only have one life and one love. What choice do I have, other than to give in to it?

"You haven't called," I say, daring to peek around my shoulder and look him in the eye. "I thought you might, but you haven't called once."

His jaw clenches once as he swallows thickly. "I didn't know what to say ... I still don't. All I know is that I wanted to see you."

Shock runs through my body at the sound of the passenger door opening and Christopher climbing in. My body's paralyzed for a moment, although my heart races recklessly. Against the stillness of everything else, the vulnerable organ rages to be heard.

The leather seat groans as Christopher takes his seat beside me, and the chill of the wind is ended with the thud of the car door closing.

For a moment, there's only silence.

"Christo—"

"I've missed you," Christopher speaks before I can finish.

With a pinch in my brow, I confuse his statement as being directed at me at first, but his gaze, a gaze that matches his brother's, is focused on the rearview mirror.

"You didn't call." His statement is more of an accusation compared to the manner in which I said it.

"You didn't call either," Cody responds with more nonchalance than I could have imagined. It's surreal being in one space with the both of them. I dream of it often. Of each of us well in all ways and able to be in one space together. Two brothers separated, both put through a different kind of hell. One more so than the other, far too early in life.

But don't they both deserve a happy ending? Wouldn't it be better for them to be together again? To lean on one another?

Easing back into my seat, I turn easily, my hand gripping the warm leather where the heater blows and I stare back at Cody to explain. "I thought you might need some space and time, so I didn't ..." I can't finish the thought. Tears prick my eyes and my voice is tight as I practically beg him, "You could always come with us." It's both an offer of peace and an offer for happiness.

"It's not—"

"And watch you and him?" Cody's voice cracks, and his gaze shifts from me to his brother. "Watch you love her like I should have?"

Christopher is silent as the tension thickens in the

small space.

"Cody," I say and my voice is pleading. "You know it could never work between us. Not after everything."

Hanging his head slightly, Cody's strong grip finds his chin as his gaze finds the back of my car seat.

"I didn't think it would end like this." Christopher's voice is low and apologetic. "When I," he pauses to clear his throat and the man I know to be weak in ways most won't admit, confesses something out loud that he's only whispered to me late at night when he thinks I'm sleeping. "When I put you two together, I thought you would take care of her. Look after her. I thought you needed each other."

"You didn't think I'd fall for her?" The allegation is clear in Cody's voice and Christopher's response doesn't come with hesitation.

"I didn't think about love at all." The declaration comes with distaste and then his voice lowers when he adds, "I knew nothing of it."

It's quiet again for a long moment, a moment in which I can barely breathe as I look between the two broken men. One with fresh wounds still bleeding, and the other with deep scars that will never fully go away.

"I missed you too ... both of you." Cody reaches for the handle of the car the moment the last word is spoken.

"Wait," Christopher yells out, far too loud in the cabin of the car, but it keeps Cody from leaving, although he's already pulled the handle and the hiss of the wind can be heard. "You should call. Soon. If you need me, you should call or write."

Cody nods and I find my goodbye trapped at the back of my throat, tears pricking as the three words beg to be spoken. *I love you.*

I still love him, but it's not my love he needs.

"We'll speak soon," is all Cody says before leaving us alone in the car. All I can do is watch his back in the side mirror as he walks away.

I don't even realize I'm crying until Christopher brushes away the tears. It's then that I recognize the hot sensation and the taste of salt.

I lose myself to the sorrow of loss, even as Christopher holds me, as he shushes me, his arm rubbing against my hair. My strong, broken man attempts to rock me and I let him, until he whispers, "I will never keep you from anything. You can always leave. I know—"

"Don't you dare," I reprimand him, not an ounce of me calm and my breathing coming out erratically. "I would never, and you better never leave me either."

I would die a lonely death if ever he left my side. Whether my lungs still moved and my heart still beat, a piece of me would crumble to ash.

"As if I could ever leave you. Little mouse, you are my only obsession."

Grabbing his hand in mine, I pull it in close to my chest

and rest my head beneath his chin. "I love you," I whisper against his chest, breathing in his masculine scent that lures me to bed every night and listening to the steady beat of his heart he once denied.

"I love you."

Chapter 22

Marcus

Her fingers slip between mine, delicate and warm against the scars of my past and the roughness of callous acts that will stay with me forever.

"I already miss him," Delilah says to me. Her gaze stays fixed ahead with the admission, past the streetlights and vacant sidewalks of this Podunk town.

"You miss everyone," I say, offering her a truth. She hasn't seen her sister and stopped speaking to her altogether when Cadence begged her to go to therapy. I think one day she'll cave to it. I think it would help her more than anything and if my information serves me right, there may be information to gather at that Rockford Center that her sister works at. All in due time, though. Right now it's only the two of us and we can take as much time as we need.

Her long lashes flutter and her beautiful amber gaze meets mine for the first time since we drove out of that parking lot. "I know you mean that I miss my sister."

A short, low grunt vibrates up my throat in confirmation.

"She just doesn't understand." Her words hold both disappointment and heartache. "None of them do."

I nod in agreement. We've had this conversation more than once. It's not their fault that they don't understand. How could they?

"I wish you'd smile," I whisper to her, bringing her hand she placed in mine to my lips. With a single kiss of her knuckles, warmth floods my chest. She smiles. A beautiful smile that belongs there on her pouty lips. I'm not sure when the cracked pieces slipped into place seemingly effortlessly, but it's the smile I could have focused on. The bits of happy before the nightmare sets in.

I want it. Cravings for more of it tempt me every day.

"I'll smile when you smile, Christopher," she answers me, the simper still playing along kissable lips.

My name felt like a curse for so long, burdened by the weight of a past that sat on my shoulders, dictating my thoughts in dark whispers of remembrance. When she says it, though, with that pained voice, it echoes forgiveness and so much more than that.

It's like a second chance. If I can only live up to what lies between the two of us, everything else drowns itself in a haze of dark fog when she says my name.

"I love it when you smile too, you know?" Delilah adds, slowing down at a red light and leaning back in her seat. Her small hand rests against her cheek as she closes her eyes. I imagine she sees him there, my brother.

"He wasn't smiling," I comment beneath my breath and it's my turn to stare past the solid red light although no cars pass in front of us. The dread of knowing his pain overwhelms me. To love someone so desperately, but let her slip through fingers that cannot contain her.

"He'll smile again." Her confidence comes with a pat of her hand over mine. Squeezing my fingers, she adds, "I have faith."

I've wondered if I'd stolen this beautiful little mouse from him. If something about me tainted her. But then I remember everything. Every piece of this puzzle that built the picture of us. I don't feel guilty for taking her. I'm sorry I didn't claim her as my own long ago.

She was always meant for me. Nothing else resonates with my intuition. There is no rhyme or reason to life, nothing fate could ensure that makes logical sense as to how I else would end up in bed with Delilah every night. My thumb resting against her bottom lip before kissing her every night so she may sleep deeply and dream of sweeter things than I have to offer.

She was meant for me, and I was meant for her. Life isn't

fair like that, but I happily accept its offer.

In return, she has all of me. I have a beautiful woman's forgiveness, her love and her life. I'll keep it safe, forevermore.

"I love you," I admit to her again. She says it far more than I do. "I love you more than anything." If it weren't the truth, I wouldn't be here with her. Starting over, spending a quiet life together with only us. She knows that.

Bad men always lose and I lost myself to her. It's a fair trade and one I'd make ten times over.

"And I love you the most," she tells me. I know that it's true. It might hurt her, maybe even both of us, but I need her and she loves me the most.

Cody

Weeks later ...

It's far too quiet to keep the thoughts away. The memories come and go as easily as the breeze whipping across my face in the pitch-black night. There isn't a star in sight, nothing but the faint lights from Jackson Street peeking through the thicket of pine trees lining the empty playground. The muted creak of the swings blowing in the wind is my only companion.

Unless I count the moments that flicker in my mind. Every single time I could have made a different choice. Every moment I questioned myself.

Every kiss from Delilah and even before that. Her accidental, delicate touches that sent blazes of heat through me when I first I met her. The stolen glances and tension I ignored for too long. Regret balances in front of me, dancing from the children's playthings as if it knew all along I'd end up here: alone and hating my silence.

If I could go back ... The thought lingers but doesn't complete itself. I'm not sure where I'd go back to. Which moment I regret the most. Back to the very beginning I suppose, to the moment my brother and I were separated. Maybe to the night my parents left our home for the last time before the accident.

With a shaky breath, my lungs fill with a bitter chill that freezes every inch of me. The moment my eyes close, the faint click of incoming footsteps has every nerve ending on high alert. Someone's coming, judging by the feminine thud of heels against the lightly dusted sidewalk. The snow won't stick, but the moments will. Memories never leave us. They're what make us who we are.

With my head back, I take a deeper breath, waiting for whoever it is to walk on by and keep going. To ignore me and leave me to this misery I've created for myself.

But the heels stop directly in front of me as the hammer of a gun is cocked. The sound echoes loudly in my mind.

"You're Marcus," a woman's voice says, although it sounds like she isn't confident in that accusation. Slowly, my eyes open to see a pale blue trench coat hanging from a brunette's slim frame. Her eyes reflect the colors of the forest, a stunning hazel, but more than that, terror.

My leather coat rustles as I lean forward, ignoring the pistol pointed at my head only two feet from me.

I could easily throw her to the ground before that trigger would be pulled. I could disarm her. I could do anything at all but sit here in silence, waiting to see what she'll do.

When she clears her throat, the uncertainty comes in thicker. Her voice wavers as she repeats, "You're Marcus."

I simply stare back at her in silence. No one knows who Marcus is. Not a soul. I found the note Christopher left for me. I've exchanged a few messages with his contact Riggins. But as far as anyone knows, Marcus died and was buried with Herman, plus Delilah's father.

"I know you are," she adds, refuting my unspoken thoughts. "You're Marcus and I need your help." Swallowing thickly, her fear permeates the air around her and her hand holding the gun trembles.

"You need my help?" I question her, feeling a heat ignite in my blood, the chill I've felt in the days past slipping away.

"Yes. Please," she begs and then she shudders. "My name

is Evalina Talvery." Her confession sends a prick down my neck. The wife to the head of one of the most violent crime families that's ever lived. I know all about the Talverys and their dealings. I know her husband and I've even heard of her daughter and the rumors about her. "I need help. You can help me," she whispers the last words and they're barely heard before being carried off in the chill of the night.

"Please. I know you're Marcus, I saw you," she says, accusing me yet again.

I could so easily help her in the way I've been trained by the FBI, taking her in and providing protection. But it only takes one look at this woman, hardened by what she's seen, and I'm certain she'd never have gone to Cody Walsh. No, no.

"Please. I have a daughter, Aria." Her bottom lip wavers, but the glare in her eyes betrays the sadness she wishes to portray. "You have to help me. Please, help me. I can give you information."

Christopher said if I needed anything, he'd come back and help. He promised he would in that note he left. He can show me how it's done.

Leaning back, I stare at the end of the pistol and speak words maybe I knew one day I'd admit, "Yes, I am Marcus."

THE THIS LOVE HURTS TRILOGY IS, IN TIMELINE, THE FIRST TRILOGY SET IN THE MERCILESS WORLD.

About the Author

Thank you so much for reading my romances. I'm just a stay at home Mom and an avid reader turned Author and I couldn't be happier.

I hope you love my books as much as I do!

More by Willow Winters
www.willowwinterswrites.com/books

Printed in Great Britain
by Amazon